# THE FREEZIES

Farrukh Dhondy

# THE FREEZIES

**TRADEWIND BOOKS**
Vancouver • London

To Zai and Aurelia—FD

# 1
## KAI'S STORY
# THE FREEZIES

*"If you're lying about a lie, are you telling the truth?"*
—Kai's dad's question

The name is Bond—Kai Bond. 008888888 . . . (recurring).
Actually, no it isn't. It's Kai Armstrong. And I'm going to
start this book, like, write the first chapter, because I pulled
the short straw. It wasn't a straw but a strip of paper held in
Sully's fist.

Sully's actually Suleikha—one of us three Freezies. The other
is Leonard, known as Leo. I can't shorten the name Kai. I guess
I could be called "K," but that could get me mistaken for a girl.

I'm going to tell you who we all are, but let me start by telling
you what I saw that day while I was walking to school. As I do
every morning, I crossed the common we call the Mead, a big
grassy patch on the lower slope of the hill, with all our houses
behind it. A path runs round it like the seam on a tennis ball.
You start at one place and then go across in a kind of figure eight
and come back to the same spot. In early March, when it rains
and rains, the path gets muddy. What I saw there that morning
wasn't there before. It was a battered old American school bus

with a trailer attached that had driven off the road and parked in the middle of the Mead. Cars aren't allowed on the Mead. So what was this rattletrap doing there? As I passed it, I heard some music. I peeked in a trailer window and saw a man playing a violin. Weird. I was late for school, so I didn't hang about.

Sul and Leo were waiting for me at the school gate, and the buzzer was just going off.

"Some geezer's driven a bus onto the Mead," I said. "I heard him playing the violin."

"Did you have drugs for breakfast?" Leo asked.

"Let's walk there after school," I said, "and see if it's still there."

But Leo said his mum would be driving him into Salton for his violin lesson, and Sul said she had to walk into the village to get the keys to her house from her mum, who was at work in the supermarket.

The three of us make up our group, which we call the Freezies. We call ourselves that to stand out in contrast to the Hotshots, a bunch of bullies who think they're hotshots. They were started by Jason, one of our classmates. They think they're so hard.

I was a member of the Hotshots once, but got thrown out. It was just jealousy on account of me scoring more goals than Jason on sports day. He started shoving me, saying I fouled him over and over, even though I never did. For revenge I wrote a rap on the Hotshots' WhatsApp group.

*You think you're a hotshot and pose like a star*
*But you're cold as a lolly, you'll never go far*

*You'll melt in your wrapper, coz you're a real drip*
*You feel you're so hard, but you can't get a grip*

*They don't see you're a loser—the Hotshots are dumb*
*But that's what you are, just leftover scum.*

The next day in the playground, one of the kids was sent to tell me that I was "frozen," which is what they say when they kick you out of their WhatsApp groups and stuff.

That's when I teamed up with Leo. He was playing squash against the library wall with a text book as the bat, and I joined in. We became friends and he asked me why I wasn't with the Hotshots anymore. I told him and he shrugged.

The same kind of thing happened to Sully. I noticed her because she was sort of aloof. We weren't friends or anything even though her Indian parents would always invite the whole class on her birthday and other times too. Lots of us—Jason and all the Hotshots and the girls who call themselves the Celebeauties—would go to her house, and her mum would serve Indian snacks, which some of the kids wouldn't touch, though they'd gobble the cake and ice cream. If I were Sully's mum, I'd be like insulted, but she didn't seem to care.

Sully—Suleikha—is a bit of a loner. What my dad, Gordon, calls an "individualist." If boys were playing football in the play-ground, she'd charge in randomly, kick the ball and run off again.

Maybe just to be cruel, the Celebeauties asked Suleikha if she wanted to join their group. She said she'd try it, but they said she had to pass some tests—like get a hair cut and wear jeans and T-shirts and not the Indian clothes she wore around the village. She told them to F off, and soon after that, three of the Celebeauties found the wheels flat on their bicycles.

So one day, four of them attacked her in the playground— pulled her hair and kicked her in the shins. Leo and I saw it and stopped them flat out.

That was when Sully, without really making it official, joined us and we thought of our name, the Freezies.

When the buzzer went for the end of school that day, I had to walk past the bus alone. The door to the trailer was open, and I saw a man lying on the floor inside with his head under what looked like a strange piano, like a small keyboard thing, but with three keyboards in steps. He was fiddling around under it and poked his head out when he saw me.

"Hello," he said. "Do you know what this is?"

He had a foreign accent.

"It's a keyboard thing, isn't it?"

"It's a harpsichord. Very rare. An antique."

"What are you doing under it?"

"Fixing it. It had fallen apart." He was getting out from where he had been lying, holding tools in his hands.

"Can you play it?" I asked.

"Sure, when it's fixed and tuned. I'll play it for you. What's your name?"

"Kai."

"Going home from school?"

"Yeah. I heard you playing the violin this morning."

"I was entertaining myself," he said. "I rolled into your village last night and had to stop. I was getting low on petrol."

I didn't know what to say to that, so I just said, "Right, got to get home. Mum will be waiting."

"Of course," he said and went back under the thing he was fixing.

Did I think we'd get involved with the man on the common? At the time I just thought he would hit the trail. He didn't—and that's why the real story begins with Leo's chapter.

## 2
### LEONARD'S TALE
# THE TRAILER ON THE COMMON

**I**'d better tell you why we are writing this story. Kai's dad, Gordon, who writes things in the newspapers, writes books with his name on the covers and is quite famous, told us to write down everything that happened, and then *tell it like a story*.

So here goes my bit. I'll start by explaining who we are.

First there's Kai. He's the cleverest of us Freezies. Kai's got a whole collection of rap on his phone and computer—people like Stormzy and Westrnmusic. He writes rap too, and he's good at school. He came first in science, and he even has a chemistry set. He says he's learning Spanish from a teach-yourself book because his folks are planning to buy a house in Spain for vacations. His dad is Jamaican, and his mum, Alexandra, is Polish. She doesn't like his rap poems. She's an actress in real plays at the Wilde Theatre in Salton. Kai acts too. They were both in *Androcles and the Lion*. Kai didn't want to be in it, but she dragged him along. Kai played Androcles, who helped a lion who had a thorn stuck in its foot, but it was a comedy, so the lion kept making jokes about it. And there were two Androcles. One was a grown-up and was kinda making a joke out of being gay, always clucking his tongue and saying "ooooo" and fluttering his eyes. Miss Honey, our drama teacher at school, came to see the play and said it was a stereotype and not funny at all, but then Kai said the audience laughed every time.

But I shouldn't just be going on and on. I need to stick to the story.

Then there's Sully, who is—I am sorry but there are no other words—skinny as a broomstick, and she never tidies her thick black hair. Suleikha says her dad won't let her cut it. He's Indian, and his religion says girls have to grow their hair and can only chop it off when their husband dies. And she's quite rude. She mutters sarcastic things under her breath when people are speaking. Her dad taught her to play Indian drums, but she prefers to play the mouth organ, and then her mum got some random fellow to teach her the flute, so that's what she does.

Her dad, Mr Sirish Rao, works in the post office, and they live in a cottage just beyond our house. It's a sort of modern cottage. Her dad's dad, Sul says, fought in the Second World War and then came here to Britain after. Her dad's crazy about cricket and football, and their front room is full of signed pictures of Indian cricketers. Her mum is always working on the computer. I think she reports for a newspaper or something in India, even though she works in the supermarket.

And finally there's me, Leo. Now I can tell you about this morning, the day after Kai told me and Sully about the bus on the Mead. My mum is what my dad calls a high-flying barrister. Every morning she's off to London by the train from Bimbury to do cases at the courts. So she gets up at six—even though it makes her as bad tempered as a batted bee—and after bumbling about and waking up Dad and trashing him for never doing any housework, she goes jogging around the Mead. Mum thinks if she jogs every morning, the fat will fall off in blobs and she'll miraculously be thin.

After Mum got back from her jog, panting and puffing, followed by our dog, Jumper, she said to no one in particular but expecting me and Dad and Gabriella, who was coming downstairs rubbing her eyes, to hear, "There's a battered old truck thing with a filthy trailer on the Mead."

"Have some coffee," my dad said, putting Jumper's food in his dish. "You're beginning to see things. There are no roads on the Mead."

He was struggling to brush the knots in Gabriella's hair, which really hurts her. Mum won't allow anyone to call her Gabby, though that's what everyone outside the house and in her preschool calls her. But Dad, he's like indifferent to children's pain. Mum says to get her hair cut and be done with it. But Dad and Gabby like her hair long.

That morning, Gabriella's nanny, Katrina, pulled up on her bike. She takes Gabriella to and from school and takes care of her after school till Dad gets home. I sometimes walk to school with them, as I did that morning.

When we set off, Katrina, who speaks with an accent, said, "Leonard, there iss lotto poliss on the Meat and they have harest some man." She can't say *mead*, but I get it all. I love the way she speaks.

As we walked past, with Katrina pushing her bike, we spotted two police cars parked on the road off the Mead.

"Kai told us about that guy," I said.

Katrina said she didn't want to know because she's not nosey. Though actually she is and knows all sorts of things about people in the village, which she reports to Mum.

I went over to the trailer and peered in the window. It was neat inside with a bed and kitchen and a door to what must have been the toilet. And yes, there was a sort of small piano and a violin and some other musical instruments on top of the piano. They took up a lot of the space.

I didn't say anything to my parents, but the next morning when my mum came back from her jog with Jumper, she said that some people from the other side of the Mead were taking pictures of the man in the trailer because they didn't like him being there. She said he was standing in his trailer door staring at them.

"What did you do?" Dad asked.

"I waved to him. He doesn't look like a traveller, and he's all alone."

"I think they should leave him alone," said Dad.

As Mum left to change out of her tracksuit and get a towel, the doorbell rang. At the door stood a man holding a plastic bucket. Jumper started barking. "Quiet, Jumper!" Dad called out.

"I am Christaki, from the trailer," he said to my dad. He had white streaks in his long hair that fell over his forehead and over his eyes. He kept brushing it back.

"I apologize for following your daughter from her morning run, but I am in desperate need of some water. If I could take some from your garden tap I'd be . . ."

"Oh sure," Dad said. He was grinning, and I knew it was because he thought it was funny that the man called Mum his daughter. "Let me show you."

"Don't make her late for school," Mum shouted from the bathroom. She had the bath running, so she hadn't heard anyone coming in. She rushed into the kitchen, wearing only her tracksuit top and undies. She saw the man, blushed and rushed back to the bathroom.

"God's truth," Dad said.

"Please don't bother to come out. I know where the tap is," Mr Christaki said, pretending he hadn't seen Mum.

"So the police haven't moved you on?" Dad asked.

"Yes, they told me to go, but I am not ready yet. They gave me twenty-four hours—and I gave them my back." He laughed at his own joke. He was pretending to be jolly, but I could tell he was sad. Not sad sad, just sad, like wondering and worried.

"I am a lawyer," Dad said. "Have they shown you a magistrate's order?"

"No, but they took me to the police station, asked questions and looked at my papers."

That day was Katrina's day off, so Dad walked Gabby and me to school. Walking past Mr Christaki's trailer, Dad said, "He's taken the bloody wheels off. That's canny."

"So he's stuck," Gabby chirped.

"You're really sharp and on the ball today, Gabs," I said.

Gabby kicked me and gave me a look. I have to remember not to be smart with her. She's smarter than me. She asks questions that I don't have answers to—like, "Leo (or Daddy), how far do you think people's eyes can see?" And if I say "Ten miles" just to keep her quiet, she'll say "Then why can we see the moon?"

That afternoon as we came out of school, Kai's mum got hold of me. She had been chatting to the others at the gate on the common, which is another piece of grass, not to be confused with the Mead. This one is bordered by trees, and it's where the school and the church are. On the other side, on the road to Salton, which is the nearest town, there's the pub, The Hautboy. Everyone calls it The Hotty, but Dad says it should be renamed The Oboe. He is annoying because he repeats the same thing every time someone mentions the stupid pub. It has a picture of a girl wearing a bonnet and a tight-fitting dress and playing an oboe, and Dad says that's why the locals call it The Hotty. Mum always gives him sharp looks and that.

"Your mother called to say your au pair, the girl from Croatia, has gone into town and can't pick you up today," Kai's mum told me. "So both of you are coming with us. Till your mum or dad picks you up. Suleikha can come too, if she wants."

Jason's mum came up. "I wanted to collar you, since you live right on the Mead. Some concerned people want to have a meeting to discuss the squatters and trailers. We wonder if we could come to your place to discuss it." There was only one trailer, but no one pointed that out.

Kai's mum said, "I suppose."

"Your place is central. It would only be for a half-hour or so. Great."

Kai's house is just beyond ours, right on top of the hill. It's a small cottage and the road turns down from there. By the time we arrived, cars were parked down the lane and people were hanging around outside the gate. Kai's mum got her keys out and let them all into the house. We were sent off with biscuits to occupy ourselves outside, but we could hear what they were saying through the open window.

The meeting was about evicting Mr Christaki and his bus and his trailer and his bucket from the Mead, making him leave town.

What happened next was quite startling. Kai's dad came home. We heard some arguments and shouting and then all the people who had been complaining about the trailer on the Mead suddenly left the house. Kai's dad stood in the doorway and shouted at them. He didn't sound very polite. A man in a brown suit yelled "Do-gooder!" on his way out.

"Your dad's furious," I said to Kai.

"Nasty people," Sul scoffed. "That fellow in the brown suit is Mr Hamilton, the editor of the *Salton Weekly*. My dad pointed him out to me one day. He wrote an editorial saying the post office in Jolyton should close as the Salton post office was so close anyway." See, Sully's dad works in the Jolyton post office, so naturally she and her family didn't like what the stupid paper wrote.

"Mum had no idea what these people were up to," Kai said. But Sul wasn't paying attention. I could see she was thinking up something.

Then she took charge—as Sul does. We were just outside Kai's house as the people began to come out. She said we should follow them to their cars and take snaps on our phones of their cars and their number plates.

We did that, and after the cars had driven away, we went into Kai's house. Kai's mum was sitting on the couch with her hands on her face. "You should have figured what they were up to," his dad was saying to her.

That's when my mum turned up, frowning. Jumper was tied to the front gate.

"Sorry to barge in and out," she said, grabbing Gabby. "I'll talk to you later, Alexandra. Come along, Leonard."

On the way home she remarked, "I wonder why Kai's mum invited those people to their house?"

At dinner Dad told Mum what he saw as he drove past Kai's house on the way home from the office. "They were getting into their cars like a cavalcade. I've seen one or two of the men in The Oboe. They're from Dewthorpe." That's the next town over. "How could she allow that meeting in her house?"

"Alexandra must have been tricked into having a meeting at her place," Mum said. "You know how generous she is. I wonder why they don't leave the poor man alone."

"Where does Mr Christaki go to the toilet?" Gabby interrupted.

"In the woods, like the bears, when no one's looking," I answered.

"He has a toilet in his trailer," Mum said.

"What happens when it gets full?" I asked.

"Oh yeeeeeeeeaaaah," Gabby joined in, "what happens then?"

"I don't wish to discuss Mr Christaki's toilet, if you don't mind, Gabriella, and you, Leonard," Mum said, using our names like she does when she wants to get all businessy.

"Leo started it," Gabby said.

"It's a chemical toilet," Dad said.

Jumper followed me out of room. "Make sure you switch off your phone and iPad!" Mum called after me. Then I heard her say to Dad, "Well, I suppose Alexandra thinks we could get squatters and all sorts, if we allow it."

After brushing my teeth, I went downstairs and poked my head round the kitchen door. Mum and Dad were drinking wine.

"We can't chase him out, Dad."

"No, Leo, we can't. And perhaps we can do better than not chase him."

"Don't even go there," Mum said. "We've got enough problems."

"We have?"

"Katrina got a letter from Croatia today. Her aunt died and left her a house on the coast, and now she's going back to fix it up, leaving us without someone to pick up Gabriella."

"Don't worry, Luciff. We'll get round it," Dad said. "I can leave the office early and work from home." Mum's name is Lucy, see, and Dad, when he's feeling wicked, says it's short for Lucifer.

"What do you mean, do better for Mr Christaki, Dad?"

"We'll look into it. Tell you tomorrow. Now please, Leo, go to bed."

Later that night I got a text from Sully. *I hope you wrote down the licence numbers of the three cars.*

The next day was Katrina's day off, so I couldn't ask her about leaving, but I did the morning after that.

"Leo, I loff you, but it is so much money to put in the drains. I cannot to give it up and the house will go to racket if I doesn't pick it up and defend it against squatters. So I loff you and Gabby, but have to leef you."

"Lobsters and crabs!" I said.

"I beg your pardons?"

"You're shellfish."

But Katrina doesn't laugh at jokes.

But she didn't 'leef' us for the next few weeks, phoning Croatia every day. When she eventually left, Mum had to ask Kai's mum and others to pick up Gabby till Dad could arrange to finish work early at Salton's only law firm.

Sully told us the next day what her plan was. We had to find the cars whose numbers we'd taken down, and then, in the evening when we were allowed out on our bikes, we'd pretend to be talking or hanging about and one of us would go near the wheel of the car where we couldn't be seen and let down the tire. She said she'd bring screwdrivers and things to poke in the valves, then press them down so air would come out. The owners would think it was a puncture and get well bothered and would have to walk or something. It was well wicked. But that was Suleikha.

Two of the cars were parked in the lane next to The Hotty, and we found another one outside Jason's house. Kai said he wanted to do that one himself. Jumper came along, but he wouldn't say anything.

The next day Sul said her dad and mum saw five or six AA cars in the village and thought something was going on. She didn't tell them anything and no one caught us.

Jason said his mum thinks whoever let the air out of the tires ought to be sent to jail. He said he knew who had let the tires down and looked at Sul. When she looked at her phone after school, she found a text that said she would be beaten up.

At school the next day, Sul told me she told her parents that Jason was sending her threatening messages. They had come to the school early that morning to speak to the principal.

Just before the bell ending the school day, Ms Husky walked in to our class. She's a tall lady with a deep voice and bunchy hair, so we call her "Shaggy." She told Jason off in front of the class and made him apologize.

Troubles come in threes. After I heard that Katrina was leaving us, the other two came on strong.

I was doing violin lessons at the time with a doddery old lady called Mrs Volta in Bimbury, which is even farther than Salton but on the other side of our village. Poor Dad has to wait outside because he says her house stinks of anti-stink. He says he'll wait in the car, but I know he sneaks off for an hour to a pub.

But this time when we got there, an ambulance was taking Mrs Volta away. Her son was at the door and told my dad that she had broken her hip and was being carted off to hospital. Dad said he was sorry and we went back home, even though he must have felt disappointed that he couldn't go to the pub.

All Mum could say was, "They should have rung and told us, to save us the trip."

Dad said we should send her flowers, and Mum agreed, though she said it was disappointing that the lessons were not happening. Not for me! It was a very jolly bye-bye to violin lessons—they were sooooooo boring. But I did feel sorry for old Mrs V.

There was no other violin teacher about. Mum tried the whole of Salton, which isn't very big, and Bimbury, without any luck.

Anyway, the third disaster happened almost immediately after that. It started in the middle of the night. I heard the noise because it woke me. Voices were coming from the Mead. Jumper heard them too and began barking.

Then I heard Dad's voice. He was still awake, and as I got out of bed, I heard him go out. I went downstairs.

"Get back to bed, darling. Dad's just gone to see what's going on," Mum said.

The angry voices were too far away for us to know what they were shouting, but we knew they were against Mr Christaki. I went back up but stayed awake. Mum went into Gabriella's room to see if she had been wakened by the noise. Then I heard Dad come back and Jumper bark loudly.

"Nasty pieces of work," Dad was saying. "Haven't seen their faces round here. From the other side of the village or probably from farther afield. They don't even live round the Mead."

"What were they shouting?"

"They surrounded Christaki's bus and trailer, banging on the sides and shouting that he had no business squatting in the village."

"Alexandra wasn't there, was she?"

"No, no. Their spokesman was a tall guy in a massive sweater. They had that Mr Hamilton from the *Salton Weekly* with them."

"What did you do?"

"I warned them that they were breaking the law, scaring someone like that. Then Jumper started barking, so they picked up and left. I was relieved, quite frankly."

"Did you see him at all? Christaki?"

"I knocked at his door and said, 'It's Greg, the person with the water tap.' When he heard that, he came out. He grabbed my hand."

"Oh God! What did he say?"

"He was very grateful. He told me that the police had given him till tomorrow to move on. Their patience had run out and they were getting an order from the county court."

Mum and Dad went up to bed and I couldn't hear any more. I was thinking about Mr Christaki being rocked inside his trailer like that and everything falling off the tables and crashing.

No more sounds that night. Only owls. Two of them live in the trees behind the house and at night they catch mice, swooping down like in the horror films. Dad took me out once with a torch and when the owl saw the light, it dropped a mouse at my feet and it ran away. Not the owl, the mouse.

The next day was Saturday. Mum went out early to jog with Jumper. Gabby and I were eating breakfast and Dad was sipping his tea when she came back, sweating and breathing hard.

"I've had a word with him. Absolutely fantastic. I had to. I was worried," she said.

"Who? What are we talking about?"

We sometimes have to ask her ten questions before we can get any sense out of Mum.

"Get me some tea," she said, filling Jumper's dish. Then she gobbled down a slice of toast with butter and jam, which Dad had made for himself. She says she's on a diet but she eats any slices of toast, if they're there, and digs for cheese in the fridge.

"I hope there was no butter on that," she said to everyone in the room even though she knows Dad eats it with butter.

"He's fabulous, Mr Christaki."

"Do you love him, Mum?" Gabby asked.

"No! I love Daddy, but I'm falling under a magic spell," she said.

"There's no such thing as magic," said smarmy-chops Gabby. "It's all tricks."

"Our Mr Christaki was standing on the grass at six-thirty in the morning in the soft dawn."

"Sun worship," Dad said.

"I don't want porridge," Gabby said for the eleventh time.

"No. Better. He was playing the violin. Oooooppphh. I was turned to stone."

"Petrified," I said. "That's the word . . . it was in a Greek story."

"Shooosh with your words. I just stood there. Listening. It was divine. I sat on the grass, hypnotized. I've invited him for breakfast," Mum said.

"He can have Gabby's porridge," I said. Mum didn't bother to say "Gabriella's." She was thinking of Mr Christaki.

"Poor man had a hard night."

"Breakfast? What, now?" Dad asked. "Why?"

Mum just smiled. Then the penny dropped.

"Ah! Oh! Breakfast it is!"

"Right!" Mum said. "And why the hell not? Have we found anyone better? That's if he wants to stay for a while and will take it on."

"But they're moving him on today," Dad said. "He told me."

"They can't move him on if he's on private land," Mum said. "You must know that. You're a lawyer."

"Ah, now I see what you're getting at."

"Yes!" said Mum. "You make him the offer. It will make you feel righteous." And she kissed Dad on the forehead.

Dad didn't look like he wanted to be kissed just then, but said, "Well, we do have a lot of meadow and it's doing absolutely nothing. Might as well open a trailer site."

And that's how Mr Christaki came to breakfast and ate Gabby's porridge, which was microwaved and made to look fresh for him.

On Monday morning I heard Katrina turning her key in the lock to our house. It was her last week with us before she left for Croatia.

"Katrina?" Mum said.

"I got paper for you, with picture of your house," Katrina said as she walked to the door of the kitchen. She had a newspaper in her hand. "That man . . ." she began, when Mum, knowing what this was about, got to the kitchen door and walked with her to the hall.

"Gabriella's ready to go," Mum said. "Come on, darling! And Leonard, grab your bicycle, you'd better get going or you'll be late." She took the newspaper that Katrina was offering her.

Gabby and Katrina left, and as I went out the door to get my bike, Mum handed me the paper. "Get this rubbish out of our house," she said, indicating that I should throw it in the trash bin by the Mead.

I didn't throw it away. I took the copy of the *Salton Weekly* to school.

The three of us read the front page before the bell rang. It was a report by the editor, Mr Hamilton, of what had happened the previous night on the Mead, but it was against Mr Christaki, saying: "The citizens of Jolyton are united in their opposition to squatters and travellers invading their open play spaces." Kai took the paper to show his mum and dad.

When I got home, Dad told me that Mr Christaki was going to remain in the village, and Mum said he had agreed to give me violin lessons. I found out that, after we left for school, Dad helped Mr Christaki put the wheels back on his trailer and move it onto our land.

That evening, Mr Christaki brought his violin to the house, and I had my first lesson with him. I wasn't really happy about starting violin again, but when we got going, I have to admit it was brilliant. When he came in with his violin case, Mum was all big smiles and pouring wine, but he didn't want any. He just turned to me and said, "Play!"

And when I asked, "Play what? How?"

He said, "Any way you like."

So I played "Twinkle," which Mrs Volta used to call "Piccadilly Circus," and then some harder pieces I'd practised with her.

He said I was standing wrong. I said that's how I was taught, and he said my teacher must have had something wrong with her hip. My dad, who was in the dining room, laughed out loud. Mr Christaki looked worried, so I said no, he was dead right. She did have something wrong with her hip—she had fallen and broken it.

Then he got all jolly and started getting me to lift my elbow and pull my shoulder back and all that. He said I had to bow correctly and we played the bits from *Fantasia* together with me just sight-reading.

I felt great making good sounds without even knowing I knew how to do it. He made me feel I could do it, so I did. He had this trick of making my playing sound terrific, and I soon got to know the trick. He played along with me and when I got too soft he would go loud, and if I went too loud he'd go soft, and if I messed up notes he'd start singing the tune to cover up the mistake and slow down till I caught up. When I sailed along because it all sounded very good, he'd stop and let me carry on by myself. The first lesson went really quickly, and I didn't notice that more than an hour had gone by, and we'd even given a five-minute concert at the end for Mum and Dad and Gabby.

That night just as I was about to go to bed, the doorbell rang. Mum opened the door.

"I am sorry to disturb you, ma'am." A policeman was standing there. "Inspector Grey from Salton."

"We've met before, Inspector," Dad said, moving in behind Mum.

"That trailer that's . . . er . . . moved onto your land."

"Yeah, Mr Christaki's house."

"He has moved with your consent, sir?"

"We invited him, Inspector," Mum said.

"Can I ask how long you intend him to stay?"

"Long as he likes," Dad said.

"The court has served papers on him, you know—but for his stopping on the Mead, not on your private land," Inspector Grey said. "Just checking, that's all. You know what some of the locals are like."

"I do," Dad said. "I handle their divorces."

The policeman laughed. I heard him go. Mum and Dad had stood up for Mr Christaki, and I could have given them a real bear hug.

The next day everybody in the village was talking about my dad taking the trailer man into our field. I heard the parents at the school gate, and then Mum said she heard them in the shops.

From then on we'd see Mr Christaki at a distance painting his trailer and things. He padded about in his socks with holes. We could see his toes like new potatoes. Twice a week he would put on boots and walk the distance from the corner of our large field to the house to give me music lessons.

Kai told his mum that I had a new violin teacher and how I loved it and was learning new pieces every day. See, Kai loved music and it was good that he'd left the Hotshots. I bet the Hotshots, who wouldn't know anything about classical music or even that it exists, would have given five fingers of their right hands if they could play the guitar like in a band, but none of them bothered to practise or would even admit to their parents that they wanted lessons.

So surprise, surprise, Kai's mum came to speak to my mum to see if she could speak to Mr Christaki. We went looking for him and went into his trailer for the first time.

He was doing some writing when we knocked, and he let us in. It was all very neat inside even though it was crowded with heaps of books as well as the piano and musical instruments I'd seen before. On one side, he had a big wooden box and then his bed and the basin, and Mum was right—he had a little cabin for his toilet, and a kitchen and everything. What I hadn't noticed before was a work bench on which he had put a violin held up-side down in a metal clip, with cloth around it like a bandage, as if it were trapped in an old torture instrument like the ones you see in the London Dungeon.

He said yes, he would be happy to teach Kai the violin or another instrument—he played quite a few. He told Mum that he had been in an orchestra and repaired the orchestra's in-struments. Then he said we must come again. He didn't know that Kai's mum had hosted the first committee meeting to kick him out. Or maybe he didn't care.

I started going to the trailer most days and had my lessons there too—inside if it was cold and outside when it was sunny. He told me that the violin in the torture instrument was two hundred years old. He'd bought it in London from a junk shop and was going to repair it.

Now Sully knew that Kai and I were going for lessons, and when we told her that Mr Christaki was expert at a lot of in-struments, she pestered her dad to let her go too. She said she could play the flute, but she wasn't too hot on it. She played a bit for us, and it may not have been hot, but it was cool. Sully's mum came to ask our mum, as though Mum were in charge of Mr Christaki. Mr Christaki of course agreed to teach Sully too, and that's how the Freezies became Mr Christaki's band: me on violin, Kai on piano and guitar and Lady Sully on flute and vocals—except when she played drums to accompany Kai's rap.

Mr Christaki was full of surprises. We'd got really friendly with him and it was coming up to Christmas. He said he was suspend-ing lessons for three days and disappearing on a little business.

He detached his little shabby bus from his trailer and drove off in it. When he came back, he took the three of us into the back to show us what he'd bought. There was a kind of piano with three keyboards, which he told us was called a harpsichord. He said it had belonged to some old church in Yorkshire where he'd been to get it, and it was busted, but he was going to sort it out. Kai said, "I saw you repairing one before."

Then one day he called at the house and gave my mum a bottle of champagne and a case of French wine. Jumper was excited to see him.

"My present for you," Mr Christaki said.

Mum looked surprised and puzzled, and I thought to myself, he doesn't have any money, what's he done? And then he told us. "Money from muck and music," he said, knowing what we both were wondering. "I sold the harpsichord. And two collectors are already bargaining for the violin."

## 3

## KAI'S STORY
# THE OZ REVOLT

I took home that newspaper from Leo, the *Salton Weekly* "rag," as my dad calls it, because of the front page article by Mr Hamilton about Mr Christaki and how he should leave the village and even the country.

I showed it to Mum first, and then Dad read over her shoulder and took it from her.

"This is exactly the opposite of what a respectable local newspaper should be saying." He jabbed his finger against the paper for emphasis. "The poor man was attacked by idiots whom he wasn't harming."

At dinner, Dad brought the paper to the table. "Kai, don't you kids play in the haunted house?"

"That was years ago, Dad," I said, making a face. "When we were kids. We don't play. We hang out or chill."

"Oh sorry, Methuselah, I thought that was your haunt. Look at this." He handed me the paper. It had a picture of what we used to call the haunted house at the bottom of the valley by the bridge across the river.

Mum came to look. The picture showed the crumbling building with its roof half gone, its windows without frames and crumbling—an empty shell of a place where we used to play hide-and-seek when we were in primary school. Beyond the haunted house, across the river, was a neat little cottage.

"That's where the lady they are calling the witch lives, isn't it?"

"She's called Callista Barr. She drives that old Morgan sports convertible you see around town. And she wears tight leather gear," Dad said. "Look at this grim headline. The *Salton Weekly* wants the haunted house demolished, saying it is a danger. The editor's a used-car con man. I don't know how he got into journalism."

"It's a village heritage site," Mum chimed in. "They can't do that."

The headline read: A Village Eyesore Should Be Demolished.

Mum took the paper from him. "You got into a run-in with her once, didn't you, Kai?"

"Her dog ran into my bike as I was crossing the bridge, and she said I ran over it. Bloody mutt! As though it was my fault. He was running madly and rammed into me and I nearly fell off. She just grabbed the dog, gave me her witch's stare and went back through her gate."

All the kids call her a witch. She lives with her two mangy dogs—not like Leo's fat dog, Jumper, who is a real tub. His mum says, "A dog starved at his master's gate predicts the ruin of something or the other." Miss Barr's house is on the river just at the end of the village near the bridge. And across the river from her house is the broken-down house the council is trying to demolish—but she won't let them because she owns it.

"You kids shouldn't hang around there. Hasn't the roof fallen in?" Dad asked. "Perhaps it should be demolished. On the other hand, maybe it can be fixed up. It's in a great location by the river. But she probably doesn't have any money for that."

As I lay in bed that night, I got the idea. I told Sul and Leo the next day. They were all for it. We agreed. Revenge on the *Salton Weekly* and its editor for telling lies about Mr Christaki. Revenge on the village for wanting to get rid of Mr Christaki. A trick to outdo all tricks.

And we put the plan into action.

Mum makes more preparations for Christmas than Santa Claus. She gets Dad to fetch all this stuff from the garden shed—lights that go off every two seconds and blare out every hour, and boxes that sing carols when we fix the dials to tell them to burst into song, and every kind of lit-up reindeer. I went to the shed and grabbed the tape recorder with a timer. I knew how to set it, but the more challenging stuff was to erase the Christmas carols from the recording in the box and rerecord the stuff I wanted.

Leo said I should ask Ajit, the IT technician at school, because he would know all about that sort of thing. I did, and Ajit said he would meet me after school in the IT room. He showed me how to take one tape out and put another tape in and said I could record whatever I liked on it.

The three of us, sitting in Leo's grand bedroom, found what

we were looking for. Wolf howls and screaming ghouls, which we copied from the computer to the tapes. After that, the light, which was easy. The Christmas gizmos I had taken from my mum's hoard could flash repeatedly and then go quiet.

We were ready.

After supper, we cycled down to the busted-up house, and I placed the equipment in rooms facing the road down to the bridge. We set the timer for all the stuff we'd recorded. The light would come on in flashes and fade and come on again.

Leo said we should wait to see who saw it as they passed, but I said, and Suleikha agreed, that we shouldn't be anywhere near the place. So we pushed off back.

The next day Leo went back straight after school and changed the batteries on the light gizmo and the sound thing. It was heavy duty—fifteen batteries each go. For three days Leo, Sully and I went there straight after school.

It hit the papers.

The headline on the front page read: PARANORMAL ACTIVITY OBSERVED BY SEVERAL WITNESSES IN HISTORIC JOLYTON HOUSE.

The article, which my dad read out loud to Mum, said that the house owned by Miss Barr was haunted. Passersby heard strange sounds coming from the house and saw flashes of light. The house had been in Miss Barr's family for generations, and tales of it being haunted by the ghosts of her ancestors had spread. One man had been murdered there, and his wife had committed suicide. His sister tragically died of heartbreak after she found out about their terrible deaths.

"These idiots fall for anything," Dad said. "But I suppose there's not much else going on in the village now that the trailer man is on Greg's private property. And he's happy with it."

No one suspected that the lights and sounds of wailing and stuff had been planted by the Freezies. Everyone was talking about the haunted house, and at school some kids said their mum or dad or grandad had passed the house at night and seen the lights and heard the sounds and reported it to the *Salton Weekly*. The newspaper said it had received reports of these lights and sounds from four different people.

"There are no such things as ghosts," we told them.

Jason said his mum was walking past there and was on the bridge when she heard the scary sounds and saw shadows passing in the window. "That house belongs to a witch and she can put all sorts of spells on it if she wants," Jason said.

I wondered whether the village would ever find out that the whole haunted business was our idea.

Mum and Mr Christaki became good friends. More and more she invited him into the house to talk the big talk about philosophy and that, and one day Mum, knowing his skills, asked him to fix an old machine that had been in the barn at the edge of the garden for a hundred years. Dad wasn't good at fixing things. Mr Christaki got quite excited by this and went out to check it. It was a machine for pulling water out of an old well. For several days he went to the shed and removed the cogs and lined up the machine piece by piece. We watched him as he scraped the cogs and dipped them in oil. Then he attached a new wooden handle and got the whole thing moving.

There is an old well beside the house, but it was closed up and grass had grown over the metal cover. I'd lived here my whole life but didn't even know it was there. Dad said Mr Christaki could dig it up if he wanted, so he did. Then, together they took the machine to the well and it was soon pulling up muddy water.

"So it's all that work for nothing," Gabby said.

"The silkworm makes silk but never wears a silk shirt," said Mr Christaki.

Soon, people in the village started bringing stuff to him to fix. Mostly it was things like the wheels of a pram, but one fellow he met in The Hotty even brought him a rusty old motorbike, which he got working in a few days. It was the way Mr C joined in and became part of the village that was so brilliant. He was really good at making friends.

## 4

## LEO'S CONTINUATION
# THE REVENGE OF MISS BARR

**D**ad came home the evening after the *Salton Weekly's* report of the haunted house and seemed quite excited. He said Miss Barr had come to the law firm where he works and said she wanted to sue the *Salton Weekly* because of the stupid report that scandalized her family. Also, people from all around were driving by the old house to see the ghosts, which of course didn't exist. She said she found various electronic lights and things in the house, and that probably the reporter had set the whole thing up to get a front page story. And now the town council was doubling its efforts to have the place demolished. It was all due to the paper and their fake story.

Miss Barr lived on her own and I always thought, when I saw her walking her two big dogs near the bridge or occasionally stopping at the village shop, that she dressed in a strange way. Sometimes she'd wear complete leather suits like a racing-car driver and sometimes she'd wear long dresses that may have looked expensive but were the opposite of her leather look. She was quite young, and if you looked at her face, you could see that she was probably younger than our mums. She drove her sports car very fast through the village, and she wasn't popular for that.

Dad told her he did think the *Salton Weekly* was a scandal sheet, and its editor was a scoundrel. He said he'd have been pleased to take up her case because, like her, he didn't believe in ghosts or haunted houses. But it would be hard to prove that the reporter had put the lights and stuff into the old house. Also it *was* derelict. He noted that maybe Mr C could fix up the old place and then she could rent it out, but Miss Barr said she didn't have the money for that.

"Are witches real?" Gabby asked, changing the subject.

Dad laughed and said, "Gabriella, I do believe in witches." He made a straight face and looked at her. Gabby turned away.

"I don't think you really believe in witches," she said.

"Of course there are no such things as witches," said Mum. "That word was just invented to be nasty to women."

Then Dad said he'd written a letter to the *Salton Weekly* on Miss Barr's behalf. The letter demanded an apology for the story and what he called "a retraction" on the front page of the paper. Dad was actually enjoying the whole thing.

"What was she like?" Mum asked.

"Not at all like a witch. Very stylish hair cut, expensive clothes."

"What do you know about expensive clothes?" Mum said, sneering.

Dad didn't bother to reply.

\*\*\*

I told Kai and Sul what had happened. It wasn't exactly what we had planned, but we had set the ball rolling. Luck was on our side, because the next day Dad came home quite excited again. He had had a response from the *Salton Weekly*, agreeing to print a story that said no ghosts were in the house, and the house was of historic value to the village. It should be saved, not destroyed.

It was then that Mr Christaki began talking about moving out of the trailer and into a house. He had read the article in the paper and, after our music lesson, asked me if I knew Miss Barr. He said he had money now from the six antique instruments he had repaired, and he needed a larger place. He could fix the roof in one day and plaster the walls and fit the windows and everything. He said he was good at that.

"So you don't mind it being haunted," I asked, jokingly.

"I'm a fixer," Mr Christaki said. "And I know a tune on the violin that makes ghosts run away." He laughed.

"Why not ask Dad to talk to Miss Barr about it. She may let you stay in the house in return for fixing it up. She doesn't want to sell it, and I am sure she'd like the haunted house rebuilt."

"For me, rebuilt is not a problem," Mr Christaki said.

Dad thought it was a good idea, and when he spoke to Miss Barr about it, she agreed to meet Mr Christaki and discuss it. I went along.

"Oh don't worry, I will start to fix the roof even tomorrow," Mr C said, pointing to some loose shingles.

Miss Barr seemed happy with that. She said if Mr Christaki was willing to fix up the old house and make it liveable, he could live in it rent-free. Mr Christaki had the skills to make it look as good as new, and Miss Barr said she was very keen for him to do it as she was fed up with living across the river from a ruin that the whole village thought was a haunted house.

Everyone was delighted, and soon after, Mr Christaki started on the repairs, taking bricks and cement and tiles and panels of pre-fab walls and timber to make new doors, all in his bus. We went over after school, and the Freezies helped him as much as we could.

After a couple of months it was done, and Mr Christaki announced he was moving. So Mum invited him to dinner again, and for the first time he dressed up. He was wearing a suit, even though it was crumpled and old. Mum made some Greek food, which I can't remember the name of, and she lit candles for the table.

The next day the trailer drove out from our drive, with Jumper barking as though he were saying goodbye. And Mr Christaki took charge of the haunted house on Water Meadow Lane. He told us he sometimes saw Miss Barr across the river and called out to say hello and she waved back.

Mr Christaki turned the front room into a music room. He even bought a larger piano and fixed it. Soon after, we started going for our lessons to Water Meadow House.

One day, Miss Barr turned up at our house, knocking on the big brass knocker on the door.

Dad answered.

"Sorry to intrude, Mr Lewis. I hope you are well? I came about the gentleman staying at Water Meadow House."

"Do come in. Yes, Christaki. Wonderful chap," Dad said.

"Teaches music to Gabby and Leonard and . . . er . . . lots of other kids in the village."

"So I hear," Miss Barr said. "Do you know where he comes from?"

"From Cyprus. But frankly I don't care and don't think anyone else should."

Miss Barr looked like she didn't think that was very friendly. But then she was hardly being Peppa Pig herself.

"I was just wondering about the legalities."

"He seems to be reliable, Miss Barr," Dad said. "He paid for the roofing materials, paint and plaster and stuff when he fixed up the house. I think you have a good neighbour."

"That's fine." Miss Barr smiled. Her face suddenly went soft. "In fact I love the music that wafts over the river."

"Why don't you ask him about himself?" Gabby said. She's so smart.

That's when Jumper ran to the window and began barking at a squirrel in the front garden.

"I am sorry to have disturbed you. Thank you, really thank you for talking to me," Miss Barr said. Then she turned, left the house and went back to her car.

Apart from being a builder and musician, Mr Christaki could fix all things. He found old junk in our sheds, stuff that no one knew was there: a cider press, an old gramophone, an ice cream-making mould and other old things. He fixed a rusty bicycle he had found somewhere—"in a dump," he said. It was an old-fashioned bike, though not a penny-farthing or anything like that. We started seeing him on his bike all over the village.

He bought yet another piano. "I buy two identical ones, like twins," he said. "Then I fix them and sell one and that pays for fixing both, and there's a lot of money left over."

"Bust up the twins? That's cruel," Sul said.

That's the sort of crazy thing she thinks about, even though she's the person who does tire terror and dreams up revenge plans.

"Not live ones like Tweedledum and Tweedledee, Sul. Just two of a kind of machine," Kai said.

"Oh," said Sully, but we knew she wasn't convinced.

Water Meadow House was now shiny and cozy. It was the music academy of the village. We thought the village had got used to Mr Christaki, now he was in the old house, but we were wrong. One morning, Mum brought the *Salton Weekly* home to show Dad. She said the paper had printed a letter signed by fifteen people against Mr Christaki. "It's shameful and disgraceful!"

Dad handed me the paper, saying, "Read why those fools object to Mr Christaki living in Water Meadow House."

The letter said:

> *Sir,*
> *It would seem that there are characters in*
> *Jolyton who encourage, invite and facilitate*
> *the invasion of this small and happy community*
> *by settlements of travellers and other people*
> *who have no roots in the village, or even in this*
> *country. As reported in your newspaper, an*
> *unprecedented number of break-ins have*

*occurred recently to houses in Jolyton and*
*surrounding villages. The police have confirmed*
*that burglaries of properties left empty while*
*families are away on holiday have increased by*
*16%. This is a lamentable fact and is clearly a*
*consequence of the do-gooders helping outsiders*
*to take up residence in a village that until*
*recently was free of crime and criminals.*

Dad said the signatures were probably fake. Two of them were "Robin Cape" and "Bartholomew Mann." Stupid made-up names. He was clearly annoyed.

"Robin Hood and Batman," I said.

"Exactly," Dad said.

I told the others about the letter and Kai said, "I think the *Salton Weekly* needs some punishment, dude."

## 5

MORE KAI

# FACE THE MUSIC

We continued with lessons even during the summer holidays. Not so many though, as Leo's family went off for three weeks to Devon, and my family went to London where we stayed with my dad's cousins. Sul stayed in the village because her dad had to work at the Salton post office.

September was soon here and the new school year began, but we hadn't forgotten about the letter in the *Salton Weekly*. We intended to take revenge but didn't know how, until some things happened that gave me a good idea.

It started when Dad brought home the *Salton Weekly* and showed me and Mum the front page.

"Look at this!" he said. "That idiot Hamilton has written an article about winning a prize for the biggest pumpkin in the Bimbury farm exhibition, and he put it on the front page of the paper!"

The photograph showed a huge pumpkin next to a statue of a tomato with a ribbon on it. A man with greased-back hair and wearing a suit was shaking hands with a grinning baldy behind the pumpkin.

"Have you come across him on your allotment?" he asked Mum.

"His allotment is nearby," Mum said. "And it's his missus that mostly does the hard work growing pumpkins. I knew they were growing huge ones because my neighbours—on the allotment, I mean—pointed it out. That's the mum of that Jason boy at Kai's school."

"That must be the same Mr Hamilton, the boss of the *Salton Weekly*, who you hate, Dad," I said.

"He came to that meeting of the villagers who are disgruntled about Mr Christaki, and he wrote the article to run him out of town. Then he printed that silly letter from Robin Hood and Batman, which was obviously an attack on your Leo's dad and maybe on me for stopping their wretched committee meeting here."

Mum interrupted him. "You know I didn't realize what they were up to, Gordon."

"Does he live in the village?" I asked.

"Outside, on Salton Road in that ugly house past the pig farm," Dad said.

That weekend, it was dinner time, when Mum came back from digging in her allotment on Barclay Fields, just beyond Water Meadow House across the bridge as the road climbs out.

"He is a bit of a show-off, your Mr Hamilton," Mum said rolling her eyes as she walked in the front door. "He's got a huge sign next to his allotment patch saying WINNER OF THE PUMPKIN PRIZE—as if anyone cares."

Dad chuckled. "A great accomplishment. Worthy of front page news, as if there's no unemployment, no flooding, no power cuts, no upcoming local elections. Just his wretched pumpkin."

"Isn't he the person who called you a do-gooder?" I asked. Dad nodded.

It was later that month when things happened at school that sparked the idea for how we could punish the *Salton Weekly*, which was so anti our Mr Christaki.

One day, Leo asked Sul and me if we'd noticed that Jason and the gang were not around the field during breaks. Usually they'd be there kicking round a ball.

"Where do they go then?" Sul asked.

"Round the back, near the teachers' car park," Leo said.

"Smoking," Sul said. "That's where the senior kids go to smoke."

Leo was right. The next day at lunch break, I followed Jason to the side entrance of the school, where the car park was. I saw them light up a joint, and they spotted me spotting them.

Jason came up to me. "If you say anything, we'll smash your face in."

"I'm terrified," I said, laughing in his face. Just then one of them, called Gerry—who isn't really one of the Hotshots—started having a coughing fit.

I scooted back and told Leo and Sul.

On the way home after school, I didn't cross the Mead but followed Gerry. I wondered why he was getting involved with the Hotbums. I walked right up next to him and he turned to look at me. He had his ear plugged and was listening to music on his phone. I gestured that he should take out the plugs.

"I didn't know you hung out with Jason's crowd?"

"Yeah, so what?"

"And smoking dope."

"Dope? No, man Kai, it was just ciggies, and I don't smoke anyway."

I raised my eyebrows.

"Anyway, they just said I had to if I wanted to join their gang."

"Why did you have to?"

"It's a test, like."

I wasn't surprised at what came next.

"Jason's big brother, Troy, the hippy with the big bike, sells dope."

"So you do smoke dope."

"Shit, bro, no. I just went along with them for a lark."

"So where's Troy get the stuff?"

"He grows it in some greenhouse or something on Wander Hill. Now leave me alone," and he put his earbuds back in.

The next day I saw Gerry and Jason and the Hotshots kicking a ball about in the playground. Gerry was looking at me more than he was at the ball. I was laughing to myself because I could tell he thought I had two holds on him. I could tell the teachers about the gang smoking pot, or I could hint to Jason that he had been gabbing about his brother, Troy, selling it.

But I wasn't thinking about either of these. A plan was forming in my mind about how to use the information Gerry had given me in a much more interesting way.

Wander Hill was the key to my plan, so after I'd told the others my idea, we started hanging out there, flying kites and playing with Jumper. And very soon we saw Troy rushing past on his bike. He parked it in front of an old broken-down greenhouse at the edge of the woods. At a distance we spotted him disappear inside for about ten minutes, come out and shoot off on his bike down the hill toward town.

As soon as he'd gone, we sauntered over to the derelict greenhouse. I stayed outside with Jumper while Sul and Leo climbed in. I could see them poking around. It wasn't long before they came back the same way.

"This is where he's growing the pot," Sul said.

"It's hidden away at the back," Leo added.

The plan was set in motion.


That Saturday afternoon the three of us rode our bikes down to Water Meadow House with Jumper running after. We asked Mr C if we could borrow a couple of spades then cycled out of the village to Wander Hill with the spades on our handle bars. We left our bikes on the road and climbed up the hillside.

Sully climbed in first. Leo followed. I stayed outside with Jumper, like before.

"Hurry up," I whispered into the old greenhouse. "Four plants are enough. Pull them out carefully with the roots."

"They're not in the ground. They are in an old bathtub sort of thing," Sul said quietly. I could barely hear her.

Just then Jumper began to bark loudly. It was Troy coming up the hill.

"Troy's coming!" I whispered, just as Leo climbed out of the broken window holding four pot plants. I quickly stashed them under a bush, but there wasn't time for Sul to climb out too before Troy got there. She was stuck inside.

I threw a stick for Jumper to chase just as Troy came up, pushing his bike. Leo and I shuffled away, acting all innocent and such. Troy glanced left and right to see if any adults were nearby. Seemingly satisfied that only two lowly Freezies and Jumper were around, he climbed in the same window Leo had climbed out of just minutes before. Then as long as it takes to tie a shoelace, Troy climbed back out, grabbed his bike and shot off down the hill.

"I hid behind some overgrown hedge kind of thing. Just in time," Sul said, climbing out the same way. "I don't think he saw me. There were lots of pot plants, so he shouldn't miss the ones we got." Sweat was pouring down her forehead even though it was a cool autumn day.

We took the plants in the saddlebags on our bikes to Water Meadow House. One light was still on, so Mr Christaki must have been in his room awake. We hid the plants in the woods behind the trailer.

Early the next morning, even before the joggers were out, Leo and I went on our bikes to pick up the plants, then crossed the bridge.

Even at that time, Miss Barr was in her garden with her two dogs, but I don't think she saw us. We went up the hill on the other side of the valley to Barclay Fields. I had taken the key to the allotment gate from the kitchen cupboard where Mum hung it up on a hook. We undid the lock and looked for Mr Hamilton's allotment. Easy. Just as Mum said, there was his WINNER sign and even a photograph and the *Salton Weekly*'s clipping stuck on a post.

We dug four holes and planted the pot plants. They were drooping a bit, so we filled a bucket at the tap and watered them as best we could. No one was around at that time. We locked the allotment gate and rode away, breaking the sound barrier with speed down the slope to the bridge.

Miss Barr was on the road, so we slowed up.

"Bicycle racers as well as musicians," she said.

"Good morning, Miss. Do your dogs bite?" Leo asked cheekily.

"Only if I tell them to attack someone," she said. "Then they maul them to death."

The dogs were sniffing aound the bridge railings for a place to pee.

"Better not cross you then, Miss," Leo shouted as we rode off.


Jolyton-cum-Barclay is full of grassers, and sure enough, one of the allotment owners phoned the police and alerted Inspector Grey about the cannabis growing in there.

Leo heard about it when his dad came home from the law firm and said the police had gone round to question Mr Hamilton.

"Dad said he'll have to explain how the plants got there," Leo told us. "Inspector Grey thinks he's hit the jackpot."

It didn't get published in the *Salton Weekly*, but everyone in the village began to talk about it.

Weeks later we heard the magistrate had let Mr Hamilton off as his wife said she tended the allotment, and hundreds of people had access to Barclay Fields allotments. Anyone could have planted them there. Mum and Dad thought it was a great joke.

No one suspected us. Revenge is sweet and butter is to eat!

And one more thing to report. Inspector Grey told my dad that when Mr Hamilton went into a pub in Salton, some regulars there started taking the piss by asking him for a packet of weed and that. So okay, we didn't get him sent to jail, but at least he was embarrassed and people began to pull his leg, and he had to sort of hide from the public.

# 6
## KAI CONTINUES
# THE SCHOOL ORCHESTRA

M r Christaki had done a lot of work on the house over the summer. It looked bigger because he had broken down walls and opened up rooms. Downstairs it felt like a recital hall.

We were getting quite good at our instruments, he told us, and one day he asked us all to come in on the same day at the same time after school.

"You all have learned to play the same piece. Now you must play it together."

As we played, he conducted me and Sul with a stick and banged on Leo's shoulder with his left hand as Leo sat at the piano. It was fantastic playing together, and we got so absorbed that we didn't notice the time until our phones started ringing to ask why we hadn't come home.

"Hand me your phone," Mr Christaki said when Leo's phone rang. He asked Leo's dad and mum to come down. They must have contacted my mum and dad and Sul's too, because all six of them were there in ten minutes.

"You are the audience," Mr Christaki said, sitting them down on an old sofa and two stiff-backed chairs. Then he made us play the whole piece again.

And that's when my mum must have got her idea.

By the time we got home, she was on about it. "Mr Christaki should be brought into school to work up an orchestra."

A few days later, Mr Christaki told me he had received an invitation from our headmistress, Mrs Husky, for tea and a chat. Mum was invited as well.

It was morning break, and I spotted Mr Christaki coming up the lane to school on his rattle-trap old bike. He'd got all dressed up, wearing a jacket and real shoes instead of his muddy old boots. Mum was waiting for him at the gate. They chatted and went inside.

The next day after school, Mr Christaki came to the playground alone. Miss Honey was there to greet him. We Freezies ran over to him, and a few other kids gathered round, even one or two of the Hotshots. Miss Honey began asking if anyone would like to be in an orchestra, and lots of kids put their hand up.

Even the idiot meathead Hotshots fell under Mr Christaki's spell, all except Jason and a few of his disciples, who went around the school saying orchestras were "saaaft," trying to imitate black accents. But boys who wouldn't stay after school to play football would stay behind to rehearse their instruments with him. I think two of them got thrown out of the Hotshots just for that. "Frozen to blood! Rasta," as my cousin Augustus, who lives in Brixton and is really cool with his dreadlocks and his electric bass guitar, would say.

And of course Miss Honey would stay behind too.

Suleikha the anti-bully is going to tell the next part.

# 7
## SULLY'S TALE
# WHAT THE DICKENS

Leo and Kai were in the orchestra, but I was in Miss Honey's after-school drama club. I would have liked to stick with them, but I couldn't do both. Miss H had this idea to do a Christmas musical with us—a new version of *Romeo and Juliet*. She had already asked Mr Christaki to write the music.

"That has all that Shakespeare stuff in it," I asked, "doesn't it?"

"No, no, no, Suleikha, not the Shakespeare version," she said. "It will be something like *West Side Story*."

Then she put on a DVD of *West Side Story* where there are two rival gangs and a girl from one falls in love with a boy from the other. "And Kai can write some rap music or grime or drill for the chorus," she said. "And the school orchestra will play the music." *A great idea*, I thought.

We all knew Kai would get the Romeo part, but when Miss Honey was making people read bits and giving out the parts, Kai wasn't at school. Miss Honey asked Leo where he was, and Leo said Kai's gran in London was very ill so the family had left to visit her the day before."

"Sully, I want you to play the Romeo part," Miss Honey said. "We are doing non-gender casting. Girls can play boys and boys can play girls."

"How will people seeing the play know, Miss?" I asked. "If Romeo's a girl and Juliet's a boy, they are still boy and girl, aren't they?"

"You'll be dressed up like a boy," she said. "That's what acting is. You can be a person different than yourself. Even very much different."

That made sense.

"If they were both boys," Jason piped in, "I wouldn't do it."

I had no idea why Jason was interested in being in the play.

"I'd do it," a boy named Todd said. Todd was the kind of boy who would do anything to get noticed.

"And who would like to audition for the part of one of the gang leaders?" Miss Honey asked.

"So that's also only for girls, Miss?" Jason asked.

"No, Jason, that can be either a boy or a girl. How about you, Leonard?"

"Sure, Miss," Leo said and made some karate gestures with his hands.

"I get it, Miss. You want soft guys to play the hard nuts, yeah?" Jason said and laughed at what he thought was a dig at Leo.

Miss Honey said, "Right, Leo, you're the gang leader, on Romeo's side, so choose a name for your gangs."

"Okay, my gang can be called the Posse," Leo said.

"My gang will be the Piranhas," said Jason.

And that was that.

"The gangs are the chorus," Miss Honey said.

"Like sing?" Jason asked.

"Maybe, or do a rap. Kai could write a rap when he gets back."

It went on like this for a couple of days—with who was going to do what role in the play. Poor Gerry was pulled in to be the police sergeant in charge of rounding up the gangs. But the trouble was that Miss Honey had not saved a good part for Kai. We knew that when he got back he'd be disappointed.

When rehearsals began, we all got scripts with our own parts highlighted. Mrs Husky turned up to watch the first rehearsal.

"Make sure you get your lines right," she said. "The bishop's coming to our Open Day, and we want to show him how good the school is."

Just like her to worry about the bishop and not care what we think.

Mr Christaki came to all the rehearsals. He was excited to be writing the music for the play, like it was a really famous telly show or something. He had six instruments to write for. Leo was the chorus lead, and I had to sing a song on my own. There was still the idea that Kai could write a rap when he got back.

When my granny died in India, I went along with Mum and Dad to the funeral. It was so sad. My cousin Salome came too. I thought about Kai's granny. I hoped she didn't die.

Whenever Mr Christaki was in the room, we noticed Miss Honey stroking her hair and pulling a strand over her left eye and kind of showing off.

One day she said, "Today we practise the theme song." The

band was there with their instruments and she asked them if they were ready.

One of the girls, Julia, said, "We're ready!" and they started to play. The others joined in. It was a song they'd changed from the original film.

*Christaki!*
*I've just met a guy named Christaki,*
*And suddenly the name*
*Will never be the same*
*To me.*

*Christaki!*
*Say it loud and it's like a magpie's clacking*
*Say it soft and it'll send the houseflies packing*
*Christaki. . .*

Miss Honey blushed full pink. "Right, that's quite enough!" she said.

Mr Christaki seemed not to notice anything, not even her posing in front of him, and started his orchestra playing while he bashed the piano. Then we sang the real song that Miss Honey had written about people being in love and hate getting in the way.

After rehearsal one day, we all signed a card for Kai about his grandma dying. None of us could think of what to write. It wasn't like it was his birthday or Christmas and it wasn't a GET WELL SOON card, because he wasn't sick and you can't say that to people whose grannies have just died.

"Just say we know she's gone to heaven," I said.

"That's juvenile, Sully. Let's be more mature," Leo said.

He was right, I suppose.

"Let's decorate it with a black border," Jason said. I was surprised that he piped in, because he wasn't the type, but then he said, "I've seen that on cards when my grandma died. That's what makes it look like it's for something sad."

"We don't want to make him more sad. We want to cheer him up," Leo suggested, "but not with funny jokes and stuff like that. Let's ask Mr Christaki."

Leo was waiting by his gate with a Batman comic. He whistled to me. Leo can whistle with two fingers between his teeth. Mr C taught him how. No one else can do it.

"Zweeeeeet!" At the signalling sound we shot down the hill.

We parked our bikes outside Mr Christaki's kitchen and went through the kitchen door, which was always wide open. Music drifted from the front room, where a window in a bay that used to be small, but that he made huge and fitted with glass, overlooked the river. He was playing the violin, a sad melody. He didn't stop till we walked through the doorway and had been standing there for half a minute. Then he must have sensed we were there, because he put down the violin and turned to us. "Ah, the two musketeers today? Did you hear my composition?"

"Did you write that?" Leo asked him. "It was very sad."

"That is accurate. That was a little bit of autobiography. A little water to sprinkle on and refresh a dried up memory."

"What were you thinking of when you wrote it?"

"I can't say exactly," he said. "Maybe about my grandfather

and a far away place where I spent many years."

"Where was that? Go on, tell us," I said.

He told us bits of his life story. But from the way he spoke I felt he didn't tell us the whole truth. I thought there had been much more, and I was right, as we later found out.

"It was my mother's dad. He went off to a place, looking for the end of the rainbow for years. Then my granny died, just like Kai's granny."

"How did she die?" Leo asked.

"She got sick and died. Just like that."

"Oh, that's sad," I said.

"Yes, it was," he said. "One place you can't find happiness is at the end of a rainbow. It's like trying to catch steam in your hand. The rainbow looks like it's ending just beyond those mountains. And people you meet on the way tell you it is just over there, just over the next hill, round the next bend. And you can look forever and ever and ever, but the real happiness is the people already around you."

"And your grandpa?"

"He found a new love. An English woman whose husband had passed away. She had no children. They were married and I had a new grandma and my mother had a new stepmother."

"Did she hate her stepmother?" I asked.

"Don't be childish, Sully," Leo said. "It's not *Cinderella*."

"She's quite right though. Like Cinderella, my mother never got on with her stepmother. But I got on with her very well, and she taught me the violin and the guitar and the piano. She taught me English too."

"Do you write sad tunes when you're feeling sad?" Leo asked.

"Did it sound sad?"

"Yes," Leo said.

"Yes," I repeated.

"Ah. The deeper currents. You heard them. Are you sad today?"

"Me? No," Leo said.

"Is that what you were thinking about, Mr Christaki, that made you so sad?" I asked him.

"That's not all," said Mr Christaki.

I glanced at Leo.

"Soon after he came back home with his new wife, my grandpa was killed."

"Killed?"

"Yes, he gave up his life for a friend."

"What do you mean?" I asked.

Mr Christaki picked up a book he had put down on his old dusty sofa. "He drew the fire," Mr Christaki said. "His life did not matter more to him than his friend. 'Greater love hath no man than that he lay down his life for his friend.'"

"And girls?" I asked.

"Yes, yes, girls too. Giving up something for a friend or taking on danger for a friend is real love."

Leo took the book from him. Mr Christaki turned the pages while the book was still in Leo's hands and pointed to a page.

"It's a far, far better thing that I do than I have ever done," Leo read.

I looked at the cover. It was called *A Tale of Two Cities*.

Leo kept it to read later.

We dropped the card at Kai's house on the way home.

\*\*\*

Leo started reading *A Tale of Two Cities* every moment he could, like he was swimming the English Channel and couldn't stop till he'd finished. Break time, class time, rehearsal time and everywhere.

But one day soon after that, Leo got a rash and didn't come to school. So after school I went to see him. He had a sign on his bedroom door saying:

YOU ARE ENTERING THE LEO-DENEO
TWINNED WITH NO-MERCY-NO-PLEO

Leo was propped up in bed reading, but with his clothes on. He had a patch of red rash on his cheek, and he showed me some of it on his arm and said it was down his back, and that it was itchy. He'd put the book down on the bed as I walked in, and now he picked it up again after his little explanation. He wanted to carry on reading even though I was there.

"Must be good then," I said.

"Better than the stuff on Netflix," he said.

"What's it about?"

"Like Mr Christaki said. It's about a man who looks like another man. It's all in London and Paris where the French are fighting a revolution. There's this beautiful girl and she loves the aristocrat."

"Does he love the girl?"

"Oh, Sully, there are all kinds of beautiful girls in long gowns, and they all get their heads chopped off."

"Anyway, are you coming down to the river?"

He said he wasn't allowed to go downstairs or out on our

bikes because he was too ill. I thought that was a feeble excuse. It was probably that he just wanted to read his book.

Leo came back to school just before Kai returned, so he was there when Mrs Husky came into our rehearsal.

"I want to say something, boys and girls," she said. "Kai will be back tomorrow. You all know that his grandmother passed away. We thought it would be best if we gave him a good part in the play. So we are in a bit of a fix. We need to find a part for him, don't we?"

"Maybe in the Posse chorus with the boys," said Miss Honey. "All the other parts have been given out, but the Posse can be of any size. That's it, I'm afraid."

"But he won't like not having any lines," Mrs Husky said.

"He can have my part. He's a better actor anyway," said Leo. "I'll be in the Posse chorus."

So that's how Kai got the role of the leader of the Posse in our play, even though he hadn't been at the audition.

Later I asked Leo why he'd been so generous.

"I knew he would be sad about his gran dying, and it wasn't his fault he couldn't be at the audition. And he's the real actor and cares about it. I'm happy with a small part."

Two days later Kai came to school. He told us how his little cousin had peed by the side of the motorway, and the wind was so strong that his mother had to hold him to stop him from blowing away. But the pee blew all over his clothes and he had to change behind the bushes.

We asked him if he saw the card and he said "Yes, thanks."

But nothing more. Maybe Mr Christaki was wrong. Maybe just knowing someone's been thinking about them doesn't cheer people up.

We told Kai about the Posse and the Piranhas, the two gangs, and I said I was in the Piranhas and the leader of the Piranhas was Gerry, and he had to get stabbed in the street by the other gang and all that.

"It's like *Romeo and Juliet*, but for today," I said.

"I've done scenes from the real *Romeo and Juliet* at the Wilde," Kai said. "I can learn lines real quick."

"Yeah, and I bet Mr C will let you make up a rap or even two," Leo suggested.

"What part did I get?" Kai asked.

Leo blurted out, "You are the leader of the other gang, the Posse. Your part is big. It's got two songs and lots of lines. I can teach you the songs straight away."

"So how does it work?"

"Rival London gangs and all about territory at first," I said. "Then a girl from one gang falls in love with a boy from the other gang. Miss Honey has made it all woke, so I'm a girl but I have the boy's name, and the boy has a girl's name. Then there's a fight and you kill Gerry. At the end, me and Simon get killed by running away and pretending to be dead. I may not have explained it too well."

"Sounds rubbish," Kai said.

It was that easy.

At rehearsal time we gathered in the hall, and Miss Honey gave Kai his script. Kai was happy with his part. Everyone was glad.

Kai changed the lyrics to make them "street." I don't think Kai ever suspected that Leo had voluntarily given up his role in the play, and no one in the cast told him.

The next day Miss Honey brought her own version of a rap that she'd written.

"That's not rap, that's crap," Jason said, and all the kids laughed.

"It's just to fill the space while Kai comes up with his version," she said.

"It's here," Kai said, handing her a piece of paper.

Miss Honey looked at it. "This is quite rude. Very rude."

"That's what grime is, Miss," Kai said.

"Please take the rude words out and the sexism too. Think of the parents who are going to be the audience. And the bishop! Change all the naughty bits."

Kai took the paper back. He was grinning.

Miss Honey went to the piano and got the other gang, the Piranhas, to rehearse the song she had written. They did, even though most of them couldn't remember the words. What a racket, man!

"There's a very dirty noise coming from this chorus," said Miss Honey. "Who's doing that?"

"It's me, Miss," Todd said. He wasn't even in the Piranhas. Todd will admit to anything, even if he didn't do it. It's so stupid.

"It's Abe, Miss," one of the girls in the chorus said. "He doesn't want to sing that rap stuff, so he's singing something else."

"And what are you singing then, Abe?"

"Miss, my grandad said that doing plays about gangs only encourages kids to do that stuff," he answered. "You know, drugs and stabbings and that. And he said rap isn't music, it's just nonsense."

"That's old fashioned of your grandpa," Miss Honey said. "And rap is a form of poetry, whatever your grandad thinks, Abraham. And we are not saying in the play we approve of gangs stabbing each other, but that's what they do, and I hope our play teaches people that it leads to tragedy."

"My grandad said a proper school should be ashamed of doing plays about gangs and stabbing with knives, Miss."

"Did he now? So what were you singing just then, Abraham?"

"I was singing 'Onward, Christian Soldiers,' Miss," Abe said. The other boys laughed.

"So you don't want to be in the play?"

"No, Miss. My grandad says Christians shouldn't believe in gangs and revenge and boys and girls running away with each other."

The day of the performance arrived and so did the bishop. Mrs Husky brought him to our English class. He was wearing a white collar and a gold cross. He had a bald head with a little fluff of white hair on the side and back.

"Please get on with whatever you are doing," Mrs Husky said.

The bishop leaned over Jason's desk. "And what is it you are writing, my boy?" he asked.

But Jason's eyes were on the golden cross that was dangling above his writing book. He stared at it. "That cross must have put you back a few bob," he said.

The bishop stepped back and coughed. "What books have you been reading?" he asked the class.

"*A Tale of Two Cities*," Leo said. "It's by Charles Dickens."

"Yes, I know it," said the bishop, turning to Leo with a gentle smile. "What did you make of it?"

"It's about greater love," Leo said.

"That it certainly is. But what does that mean?"

"Well, in the story a character called Sydney Carton loves a lady, and she loves a man called Charles Darnay, who looks like Sydney Carton, you see . . ."

"Yes, go on," said the bishop.

"And Carton sacrifices himself by taking Darnay's place on the guillotine, where they cut his head off. It's the most that anyone can do for any other human being," said Leo. "To lay down one's life for a friend."

"Yes. And for love," said the bishop.

"And that's what it means: 'Greater love hath no man,'" Leo said, just as Mr Christaki had said it. "If you are someone's friend, you can sometimes step in for them."

"That's very wise. It's from the Bible," the bishop said. "And do all of you know the book?"

"All of us," Leonard said. Which was absolutely untrue.


That evening we performed the play for the parents. It went off well and the bishop clapped. Miss Honey was delighted. Kai was very good as the leader of the Posse gang. It was like he was playing Shakespeare's Mercutio, who gets stabbed and says "a plague on both your houses." Miss Honey's version changed that to: "Your quarrels over nothing have killed me dead!"

Then the chorus began singing Kai's cleaned-up rap. They were halfway through when we heard a funny sound. Leo raised his arm and finished the real rap—the orginal one that Kai had written. It was good, so I'll tell you how it goes:

*We live on the margins coz that's how it izz*
*How we make ends meet, that's none of your bizz*
*We sell a bit of this and that to them who want to play*
*And pay the Babylonians to look the other way.*

*The judge will bang his gavel to serve a term inside*
*You give him a salute and thank him for the ride*
*I been now twice in places they keep the young offender*
*The brudders and sisters will never surrender. . .*

I played the part of Romeo, my long hair in a cap turned backward. The bishop grinned at me from the front row.

The next day Leo and Kai came pushing their bikes up the Mead road. We went down to Mr Christaki's house, where I had a flute lesson.

"Come on, I've got a new machine in the shed," Mr Christaki said. He led us to the shed and showed us a heavy metal and wood thing, with a handle and two rotating drums.

"Can you tell me what this is?" he asked.

"It's a thing to dry clothes before they had tumble dryers," Leo said.

"Not before they had the sun and the breeze," Mr Christaki said. "But that's not what we're going to use it for. Look in the sink."

In the sink were two long yellow-looking poles that had knots in them at regular intervals.

"Bamboo," said Leo.

"Not far off. Sugarcane. Got it from the Indian shop in Bimbury."

"What do you do with it?" Leo asked.

"Ach! Patience," Mr Christaki said.

He put a bowl under the two drums, pushed one of the poles of sugarcane through the mangle and turned the handle. He tightened the mangle and, sure enough, a lot of juice began to flow, white and frothy, down the clean drum. He gathered it in the bowl.

"Can I have a go?" Leo asked, and the three of us turned the handle, which was very hard. The juice came out of the sugarcane poles like a lemon being squeezed. It poured out as we turned the handle, and Mr Christaki dished it out in glasses. It was delicious, like smoothies.

"Leo told the story of greater love to the bishop," I said.

"I hope he understood," Mr Christaki said.

We went back in the house and the music room, and he brought out a tambourine. Sitting there drinking the frothy juice, we saw Miss Barr step out of her house and get into her swanky black sports car. As she got in, she turned and waved to us, neighbourly like. By the time we all waved back, she was off for a drive.

I wondered why she suddenly decided to be friendly.

# 8
## LEO AGAIN
# A PICTURE WINDOW

I'm back.

After the Christmas play, we were on school holidays. I went to Spain with my family, and Kai went to visit his Polish grandmother up north. She lives in the Lake District somewhere. Sully didn't go anywhere because her dad had to work overtime at the post office.

When school started up again, Mr Christaki said he had to go to London for a few days. We were used to him going on trips to buy broken old musical instruments from flea markets. This time he said he was going to bring back a surprise, and it wouldn't be a musical instrument either. He wouldn't tell us what it was. He asked us to tell our parents he'd be away and to bike past Water Meadow House to see that no one had broken in. We did this, and some days I saw Miss Barr walking in the garden with her dogs, staring up at Mr Christaki's house.

True to his word, Mr Christaki did bring back a fantastic surprise. It was a little girl. He said that she was four years old and her mum and dad had to travel for their job. He was going to look after her while they were gone. She was cute, with black hair in ringlets and huge eyes. Her name was Miriam. That first day, she wore a thick black-and-white dress with beautiful embroidery, but Mr C put that away and bought her a lot of clothes from the kids' shop in Bimbury.

She didn't speak much to us. Her English wasn't that good, but she could understand us. She spoke some kind of foreign language to Mr Christaki, probably Greek. But he only answered her in English.

Miriam had a mind of her own. If she liked you, she would stare with big eyes when you talked, as though really listening, and when you stopped she would hug and kiss you. If she didn't like you, she would just turn her back and stand there facing the other way. She did that to Kai at first. Then she made best friends with him.

Mr C hired Mrs Morris, who used to work as a dinner lady at school, as part-time nanny. He had so much work to do with the music lessons, fixing up old instruments and selling them, and fixing up a room for Miriam, that he needed the help. Miriam spoke with Mrs Morris in English, which she was quickly learning to speak.

For Miriam's room, Mr C smashed up the outside wall toward the river and made a big window into the garden. He painted the other walls in blue and yellow and covered them with pictures of moons and stars. We didn't know he could paint, but the pictures appeared as if by magic under his brush.

Mum gave Miriam a set of Peter Rabbit books—not the ones I had when I was small, but new ones.

But after a couple of weeks, Mum and Dad began asking me questions.

"When are Miriam's parents coming to pick her up?" Mum asked, trying to sound casual.

"Not sure," I answered.

"Something's not right," Dad said, frowning like he does when he's bothered by something.

"She needs her mother," Mum said, adding that I should tell Mr Christaki that she would pop round to help him with advice or anything else he needed.

The window in Miriam's room was finished, and we gathered there to check the view. We could see both ways down the river and into Miss Barr's beautiful house, which had six round columns holding up a room and its big curved window on the first floor. We could now look into it and straight into her kitchen downstairs, a view that was hidden before by an elm tree on our side of the river. Miss Barr's bedroom was in full view.

It didn't take her long to cross the bridge and ring the bell at Water Meadow House. We were upstairs, playing with Miriam and her basket of toys. Mr C must have had a feeling about who it was. He went downstairs but asked us to wait just there. We could hear Miss Barr being very angry. Mr Christaki was saying something but we couldn't make it out. We tried to listen, but they walked out of the house, and their voices faded. We went to the window and saw them in the garden.

Mr C picked up a stone and threw it in the stream. Then Miss Barr went away and he came back up. He looked worried. He said she was very angry that now we could see her living her life. She was demanding that Mr Christaki take down the window and rebuild the wall.

"I told her we can both now look at each other," he said, "like the spider and the fly." He was trying to make a joke, but I could see he was worried.

"That seems very fair," said Sully.

"She could have curtains," I suggested.

"She said she would complain, because I didn't have permission to make a window. Do you need permission to look out at the world? To get some light?"

"She shouldn't have secrets," Kai said.

"She's being silly," Sully said.

"She is my neighbour. We can't fight," Mr Christaki said.

Mr Christaki didn't mention Miss Barr again. He carried on as if nothing had happened. His big project now was making toys for Miriam. He took old junk like broken tape recorders out of his garage, took bits out of them and made them into moving toys with batteries: little clowns made of cans, like robots, that ran on wheels and waved their arms, which were made of old plastic toothbrushes. He made boxes that spoke, opened and closed themselves, and laughed and made music.

Very often after school we'd go to Mr Christaki's, even when none of us had a lesson. We did our homework and that at Water Meadow House. And we'd play with Miriam.

Sometimes Mr Christaki gave us lectures on stuff.

"I am going to tell you what the theory of relativity is," he said one day. "It sounds like a mountain, but it's a mushroom. Any fool who can do two plus two can understand it."

"Interesting," Kai said. But he didn't sound convinced.

"Albert Einstein figured it out about a hundred years ago."

"Okay, shoot," Sully said.

"Shoot? I don't like the sound of that."

"It just means go ahead and tell us," I explained.

"With it," Mr C continued, "Einstein proved that nothing could go faster than the speed of light."

"So Superman can't go faster," Sully said.

"Don't be stupid," Kai said.

Mr Christaki went on. "It also has to do with the different speeds of things and how they relate to each other. Take, for example, throwing stones from a train. You have to add the speed of the train to the speed of the stone. Or take it away, if you see what I mean."

"That's wicked," Sully said. "Someone could get hurt or you could hit a sheep."

He ignored her. "So the speed of light is the fastest thing in the universe."

"I told my dad the relativity theory," Kai said when we saw him at school break.

"So?" I asked.

"He says he has his own relativity theory—the fewer the relatives the better it is."

# 9
## SULLY'S TALE
# PURSUIT OF THE FLUTE

I've got to start on the day Dad lost his job. It was just after the Christmas holidays, but he didn't tell Mum or me for a week. Seeing his face when he got home from the post office, I knew something was wrong. I suppose he thought he'd find another job first and then he could break the bad news and good news at the same time. But he couldn't find a job, and he started going out and pretending he was still going to work, and he would come back in the evening after work time. But I caught him out. One day after school when I was going to Mr Christaki's, I spotted him. I think Dad saw me too because he turned and walked across the wooden bridge as though he was hiding from me.

So that night I asked him. I didn't know I was prying into his deepest worry and secret.

"Were you walking by the river today? I saw you," I said.

Dad just looked down at his shoes, and I looked at them too and then so did Mum. When Mum looks at shoes and clothes and hair and things, she notices them.

"Your shoes are mucky," she said. "Like you've been tramping through mud."

"Down by the river. Sully is right. She did see me. I . . . I just had to be by myself and think."

"Think? About what? What have you done?"

See, Mum's sharp about muddy shoes and about nits and bits in my hair or whether I've eaten a piece or two of the diet chocolate she keeps, but she's not very good at noticing Dad's moods. I knew something was up, but she hadn't noticed it.

"I'm unemployed. Out of a job. They've closed the post office. I am amazed you haven't heard."

"Of course I've heard, but you said they'd transferred you to Salton."

"Yes, that's where I go looking for a job."

"I thought the union won that fight. You told me they were shifting you all to Salton."

"I didn't want to tell you," he said. "They kept everyone on except me and Scotty. And the union wasn't willing to fight anymore."

Dad used to always boast about the union, though I don't think this union treated him very well. When he got kicked out of his job, they made some noises but he never got his job back at the post office. The truth is that Dad had tried to fight for the union leader's job and lost the vote, so the new leader didn't like him and didn't want him around. Dad says he's a socialist and that the leader they elected wasn't. He says he wants me to be a socialist too, but I said I didn't understand all of what that meant, and

Mum said it means that people should be sort of equal, and nobody should be very poor. I said I agreed with that, so I would be one when I grew up. But there was time.

Dad said he would have to go out of Jolyton and probably farther than Salton to look for a job because there was nothing he was good at. He was very sad. Still, he told us not to tell anyone. I didn't tell the Freezies anything and carried on as if nothing had happened.

Mum said she would get a job that paid more than the part-time work in the supermarket. She went to a lot of places—shops and factories—but couldn't get any work. I could tell she was getting a bit desperate when she discussed the daily disappointing round of looking for work with Dad each evening.

Dad was also looking for work but didn't find anything that he could do. He was offered a job driving a truck, but Mum didn't want him to do that as it would mean he might be away for a week at a time.

Then one day Mum came back and said she'd found a better-paying job, and it was fantastic because it was at a dry-cleaning plant as a supervisor. Dad looked as though he didn't really want to hear it, but he said she should do it till he found employment and then she could go back to writing for Indian papers as she had always done. He wouldn't have wanted her bringing money into the house when he wasn't. He even looked guilty for spending his time watching cricket and football on the telly.

I knew that both Dad and Mum were sadder and more worried than they were letting on. Dad even told Leo's dad a lie when picking me up from school one day. He said he had a new shift at work so he could pick me up instead of Mum.

"Why did you tell him lies, Dad?" I asked him.

"Because he was looking at me from his posh car and standing in his posh shoes as if he owned the bloody place. They want to know my business."

"I think you are imagining it," I said even though I thought it might be true. He gave me a strict look but said nothing. On the way home he was kind of thoughtful.

"If people think you are out of a job, they think you're worthless," he said, and I knew he was talking to himself as well as to me. Every day he sent off letters for jobs, and when the postman came he eagerly opened the envelopes, hoping someone had replied with an offer. But no one did.

One day Mum didn't come home from work, and Dad was pacing about, worried. When the phone rang, Dad picked it up, listened, then mumbled a few things into the line. He looked worried sick. He put the phone down and told me to get ready. We had to go to Bimbury hospital where my mum had been taken after an accident at work.

As we drove toward Bimbury, he said, "Don't panic. Mum's okay but she got burned."

"Burned?"

He didn't answer immediately. He looked angry. "She's been lying to us. She wasn't working as a supervisor at the plant at all. She was working on the steam irons in the laundry section but didn't want to tell me because I'd have stopped her and taken the truck-driving job."

When we got to the hospital, there were two ladies waiting for us. They asked Dad if we had come for Mrs Rao and when he said we had, they said they worked with Mum and had brought her there and she was being treated for burns, but there was nothing to worry about. Dad seemed to cool down and asked what exactly happened.

One of the ladies told him that an ironing machine had burst, and she'd got her hands and face burned by steam.

Eventually Mum came out of the treatment area all bandaged and with a plaster on her face. Her face looked patchy and dreadful, and I could tell she'd been crying. We took her home. Dad said nothing on the way back.

It was only when we got back home that he started pacing about and getting more and more angry. He didn't accuse her of lying to him about where she worked and what she did, but he said she wasn't going to do that job anymore. He called the laundry and spoke to the owner.

"He said it is Mum's fault because she hadn't followed the safety rules. That's how it is," Dad told us later.

"It was my fault," Mum acknowledged. "He's right. I was trying to hurry."

"Why were you rushing?"

"Because they pay by the weight of clothes you do, so you don't slack off, and I wanted to earn more than yesterday."

Dad looked stunned for a moment. "You should never have worked in a place without a union."

"Why are you being so nasty, Sirish?" Mum said. "What has happened to you?"

"What's happened to me is I got the sack. I worked hard, and that's what I got. And look what's happened to you. They pay you peanuts for sweated work, make thousands and say it's your fault when a machine nearly kills you. That's what's happened to us and will continue to happen to us."

"Don't exaggerate," Mum said.

Dad was in a bad mood and when I was practising on my flute he came in and asked where I had got the flute from. I said Mr Christaki knew we couldn't afford a flute so he said I could use his.

"So he thinks we are beggars," Dad said. He asked me to hand him the flute and I did.


The next day, Dad took my black flute case and went off across the hump of the hill toward Water Meadow House.

Mr Christaki came to school the next day and brought the flute with him. "Please take this home, Sully, and tell your father I apologize for anything I may have said that annoyed him."

I didn't want to take it because I knew Dad wouldn't allow it. But if I didn't take it, Mr Christaki would think I was taking Dad's side. I hid the flute in my school bag and gave it to Mum to put away somewhere so that Dad wouldn't know. Mum said she would hide it in her wardrobe.

But I didn't leave it there long because I was afraid Dad would find it. So I took the flute from Mum's wardrobe and biked down to Miss Barr's house.

"You said you liked our music so I've come with my flute," I said when she opened the door.

She looked pleased to see me and called me in and gave me a drink. I played her some pieces and she listened.

Even though I made mistakes, she clapped. She said I must come and play music again, and she wished she had a flute so she could maybe get back into playing like she did when she was young. I was looking for an excuse to ask if I could leave the flute there. "Can I leave it here? In your house?"

"Why?"

"Because it's worth a lot and our house is not safe, ma'am," I said, handing her the flute case.

I didn't know why I called her ma'am, but it was maybe because I had heard people calling the Queen that and she wasn't like a teacher, so I didn't want to call her Miss. She didn't like it though. "Oh, Sully, you mustn't call me ma'am. Please call me Callista. As you would a friend. And of course I'll keep your flute safe. Nobody comes here. Even the burglars think I am a bit of a witch and stay away." She smiled, and I smiled because I knew that it was true.

That's how I made friends with Miss Barr. She even went and bought herself a flute, and we arranged a time when we could play together. I would have told Mum and Dad where I was going, but Dad would have said he didn't want me going there as everyone in the village thought she was strange. So I said I was going to the library.

But she insisted on driving me home one day, and Dad was digging in the garden when we drove up. Miss Barr stepped out and held out her hand. "Callista Barr. I've made friends with Sully and her crowd. Charming young lady—and the lads too. So I thought it proper that I meet her parents."

Dad said she should come in for tea to thank her "for bringing our Sully home" and all that, so she did. She chatted away with my dad. He even told her he was unemployed.

"Oh that's unfortunate," she said. And they talked about politics and about the government, and they both seemed to agree even though I didn't understand what they were saying.

After that Dad said it was okay to visit her, and I went quite a few times even though Kai and Leo didn't know that I was going there.

Miss Barr—Callista—was very nice to me. And once or twice, when Dad went off looking for a job in Salton or Bimbury and Mum was busy, he would phone her and ask if she could pick me up from school. He was now going off in his bus every day.

I told the others, and they were surprised to hear that Miss Barr was quite an okay person.

# 10

## KAI'S TALE

# THE DISAPPEARANCE

A few days later when we all were hanging about at Water Meadow House, two gentlemen in suits and ties called. They were from the council. Mrs Morris let them in.

"We're looking into a complaint from a neighbour," one said to Mr Christaki.

"Ah, the window," said Mr Christaki. He took them upstairs and we went home.

The next day my violin lesson went on till late. Miriam was being put to bed and she wanted me to read a story to her. It was getting dark outside and, looking across the river, I could see that all the lights of Miss Barr's house were on. But just as Mr C turned the light on behind Miriam's big picture window, Miss Barr's lights went off. Her house was in darkness. I stood up at the picture window and looked at Miss Barr's darkened windows. That's when I thought I could see her, not through her window but under the trees on the riverbank, looking up at

Miriam's window. She was standing very still, facing us. I could only see her silhouette. Her dogs began barking from inside the house, but she didn't move.

Soon the dogs came out and began to lick her hand. It was like a shadow play. But there wasn't anything to it, really. It was her garden and her life and she could stand and stare if she liked.

Very soon after that, I was biking past Water Meadow House with Jumper. There were two men in blue suits on the porch, talking to Mr Christaki. A police car was stopped out front. I parked the bike, tied Jumper to a tree and sauntered up to the house.

"May we come in?" I heard the men ask.

I followed them inside just in time to hear one of them telling Mr Christaki to come to the station the next day with his papers. I backed out the front door, untied Jumper and sped away.

The next day when I went for my music lesson, the house was locked. I knocked and waited. Mrs Morris came to the door and handed me a note that said "*Leo, sorry*" and nothing else.

"His bus's gone," Mrs Morris said. "And so is the trailer. He must have left in quite a hurry, because he left Miriam's clothes in the cupboard. I'm sorting out the house, for when he gets back." But he didn't return. That day or the next. Mr Christaki had taken his Miriam and vanished.

On the third day we followed the tracks left by the trailer. They had gone out of the gate, turned left and past the wooden bridge. The road out of the village.

We went up to the house to say goodbye to Mrs Morris.

"I won't be coming in, now that there's no one here," she said.

There weren't any clues as to why they had gone. Water Meadow House, our house of music, was now silent. That left a big hole in our lives. Sadness. There was no cool place, without interference from bossy parents, to hang out after school. Standing in front of it, looking across the river, we saw Miss Barr at her window, a dark form, brushing her hair.

"She probably put a spell on them to make them disappear," Sully said. "All because of the picture window."

"No, Sully," Leo said. "But something's not right."

I agreed. A man and a child just disappear and don't tell anyone? Weird or what.

We went again the next day after school to see if they were back. But they weren't. The house was still empty and eerie. There was nothing we could do, so we went home for dinner.

Later that evening, I told Dad that Mr Christaki was missing and that Miss Barr knew too.

A week or so after, Leo's dad went down to the station at Salton and asked Inspector Grey if they knew anything about Mr Christaki. They told him the police in Liverpool had found the trailer. It had been abandoned and was full of Mr Christaki's stuff.

"Dad said it means Mr C is on the run," Leo said at school break. He had on his serious look. "He might vanish into thin air."

Sully came over and listened in.

"It's bad," Leo continued. "The police told my dad Mr C is an illegal immigrant, and so is Miriam."

"He's an illegal immigrant?"

"It means he's not got permission to live in England," Sully said. "He's probably got false rubbish documents and . . ."

"This is the kicker," Leo said, butting in. "The government will deport him and won't let him come back ever."

When I told Dad what Leo's dad had said, he said he already knew.

"He's made it worse for himself by running off," Dad said. "He should have stayed and appealed through the proper procedures. Greg could have found a loophole."

We got very depressed. Sully was worried that they wouldn't have any money for food, and I said, "I think Mr C can look after himself. But he should have asked for help instead of running off."

The next day, we saw two cars going toward Water Meadow House. We followed on our bikes. Jumper came bounding along after us. One of them was a police car, and the other had two men in suits and raincoats. They weren't our policemen. They went round the back and inside the house. I guess Mrs Morris had forgotten to lock the back door. We watched them through the window. They were searching the place, I suppose. When they came out, they told us to clear off.

Miss Barr came over then with her dogs. Jumper barked loudly at them.

"What are you doing going through the house?" she asked the officer. "I own it."

"We've got a court order, ma'am."

"He's probably away for a holiday," Miss Barr said. "He's got a child with him, you know."

"I doubt he'll be back, ma'am. Good evening to you."

Miss Barr turned to us. "Do you know where he's gone, Suleikha?"

It felt strange seeing Miss Barr so familiar with Sully, like she knew her well—even though Sully had told us she went to her house a few times. She sure didn't look scary close up.

"We don't know where he's gone, but they've found his trailer somewhere," I said. "That's all we know."

"Grief! He got away fast. I wonder why he has done a runner?"

"You complained about him, didn't you?" Leo said.

Afterward, we wished he hadn't said this, but at the time it came out sort of naturally. Rude, but it's what we thought.

"Now wait a minute, young man. I complained about him installing huge windows overlooking my house and looking right into my bedroom. That's all. I . . . I even went to the council and dropped the complaint. I thought he was a good neighbour, and I liked the fact that he was there. Tell you the truth, I used to sit by the window when he played music—very beautiful melancholy tunes. You know what the villagers thought. They used to say the place was haunted, before he arrived. But yes, I did complain."

She likes to talk, I was thinking, and I was right.

"I feel bad about all this. I didn't think it when he moved in, but his playing transformed this neck of the woods."

She said that with her hand on her breast. I think Miss Barr took us all by surprise. Her dogs were straining at the leash now, and she let them loose to wander by themselves. They went over to several trees and did wees against them. Jumper followed. The dogs sniffed each other, and we thought they might fight, but they didn't. Like they'd accepted Jumper as a friend—the dog triad!

"I love music," Miss Barr added.

"We know," I said. "I mean we hear you playing your CDs, opera and that."

"You play it very loud," Sully said.

"Do I? Oh dear. I suppose I got used to not having neighbours. But where do you suppose Christaki and his child have gone?"

"My dad says he might have skipped to Ireland."

"Your dad's wrong," Sully said. "You can't skip to Ireland, there's the Irish sea in between."

"Would you young gentlemen and lady care to pop back to my place for some ice cream or a drink?"

"Yeah, sure," Sully said.

We wheeled our bikes across the bridge. Miss Barr was a hermitess. Her two dogs followed us when she whistled at them through her narrow lips. Jumper came too, and Leo tied him up in the yard. Her dogs were loose, so when they came to Jumper wagging their tails, Leo let Jumper off the lead to let them all romp together.

Her lawn was wonderful, like a carpet, though I'd never seen anyone mowing it. We left our bikes on the porch and followed her into the house.

"Don't feed the vultures or gremlins," Leo whispered.

Her house was full of antiques, and one wall in the hall was just patterned old tiles. It was very clean and neat, but the chairs were old and some were cane and some were wood, and they didn't match each other. But they were good to sit on. It was the sort of room that makes you whisper, which we did when she went to fetch the ice cream.

"She's sure nice," Leo said. "She must know we feel bad about Mr C disappearing."

Miss B came back with a tray of ice cream and biscuits and crisps. As we gobbled them up, Leo told her the whole Christaki story, or what we knew of it. Miss Barr, being a hermitess, hadn't heard anything.

"The police say he's illegal," I said, "but they could be telling lies."

"That's all very sad," she said. "I am sure it's enough reason to run away if people say such things about you. I have watched them together in the garden and they were so happy together, those two."

As we were finishing the treats, Miss Barr said, "Now, boys, you must tell me your names. I am Callista."

"I am Leonard and this is Kai."

"We call ourselves the Freezies because we were—at least Kai was—frozen out of the losers' club," Sully said. "And sometimes I want us to be called the Triad, which is the Chinese word for their Mafia."

"Ah, the Mafia, the evil secret society. People in the village think I am quite evil, you know, so I'd be a good recruit for your triad. But of course I wouldn't want to muscle in. You do know what they say about me, don't you?"

We did, but we all said we didn't.

"They call me a sorceress," she said, breaking into a smile. "And the only saucer I know is what goes under the cup."

Leo and I laughed, but Sully didn't even smile.

"We play together in a band," Sully said. "But we want to do our own songs. Leo plays the piano and the viola and the violin. He is totally fossilized."

"You mean versatile," Kai said.

Miss Barr laughed.

"Kai writes damn good rap," Sully said.

"For me a triad is also three notes in a chord," Miss Barr said. "And triads are secret and evil." She gave us a wicked smile.

At that Sully got up and said, "We have to go now."

"Thank you for coming. I don't have many friends here." And then she said we shouldn't accept that silence had descended on Water Meadow House and the woods around it. We should keep Mr C's spirit in the place by bringing our musical instruments to her house and playing them.

"You see, I can't now just open the kitchen window and catch your playing from across the river. I really would love it. And you must tell me what you like to eat and I'll fetch it in."

We smiled and said we would, but I knew we wouldn't.

"I think he will be back, you know," Miss Barr shouted as we cycled out of her gate with Jumper following. We crossed the hump-backed wooden bridge and then down past the gate of Water Meadow House and up the lane and hill, home.

"I still think she's weird," I said, saying goodbye to my friends.

"She looks like she's thinking something in the back of her mind all the time," said Leo.

That night, I thought it was obvious Miss Barr had been lonely before Mr Christaki came along with his music and his little girl and our music. And I fell asleep wondering about where they had gone. When I woke up I knew what we could do to find them. Sometimes you have to go to sleep on a problem.

## 11

## KAI HOGS THE NEXT CHAPTER TOO
# WHO IS CHRISTAKI?

Rumours that Mr C had kidnapped Miriam, or that he was a terrorist, began to spread.

"We need to find them. Greg and Lucy will get them permission to stay legally," Mum said.

So they got a village committee together to work on it. Mum didn't care to recall that she had hosted the first committee to throw Mr C out. Now she was forming one to find him and bring him back. Mum's brain is a convenient one. It forgets things that she's said or done to me or to Dad when it's not convenient. It's not that she's two-faced or anything. It's just that her memory adjusts to what she wants it to.

Ten people came to the first meeting, which was at our house, because Mum had been on the phone to people every day, organizing it. The Freezies were invited too.

Dad, the philosopher, said finding Mr C posed a problem. He would want to be found by some people and not by others. Leo's mum, Lucy, was very precise in what she said because, as a QC, she knew what she said was "asylum law." We learned that that was when refugees from some kind of danger to their lives come here for protection. We all agreed that we had to somehow find Mr Christaki and Miriam and get them to apply for asylum.

After the grown-ups' meeting, the Freezies had our own meeting. I said we should try to find Mr C before the police did, and the others agreed, so we wrote an email to Mr Christaki.

*Everybody wants you to stay here and please bring back Miriam and at least give us a clue as to where you are so we can talk to you and help. Our mums and dads also want to help.*

We waited some time for a reply, but there wasn't one. So the three of us met on the banks of the river under the window of Water Meadow House to discuss what else we could do. We tried to phone Mr C, but we got a tone that said the call did not go through.

Then Leo said he had an idea.

"To help them stay hidden?" Sul asked.

"But we don't want them to stay hidden," I said. "We want to keep them here in Jolyton."

Leo ignored us and just said, "The antiques."

We didn't know what he meant, but he scrambled up and ran to the house. Mr Christaki always kept a key under a potted plant on the porch.

We all trooped into the house and then into the small room where Mr C repaired his musical insruments.

"He's taken the violin and the viola that he was fixing," Leo said, waving his hand around the room. "He'll sell them. That's the way he'll be getting money."

"The cops said where they found his trailer."

"Where?" Sul asked.

"Liverpool," Leo said.

"Right," I said. "We have to get on the computer and find all the shops in Liverpool that sell old musical instruments."

"Then get their phone numbers," Leo added, clicking his fingers. "He told me the name of the violin, it's Mitt-something."

We went over to Leo's and huddled round his computer.

"Mittenwald! That's it," Leo said.

"You are fantabulous, Lionish," Sully said. "How detectivish is that!"

We got the numbers of some shops in and around Liverpool that sold antique musical instruments. I was nominated to call them as I was the one with the deepest voice. I asked them if they had a Mittenwald viola or violin.

Yessssss! Finally the dude at the end of one of the phone calls said a man had just sold them a viola. He said the man would be coming back with a Mittenwald violin on Saturday. "Might you be interested in both?" he asked. "They are unique examples."

"Did he have a foreign accent?" I asked.

"Why yes, he did," the man answered. "Why do you ask?"

"No reason," I said. "Thanks."

So we went downstairs and told Leo's dad.

Action! Leo's dad called my dad, and they decided to drive to Liverpool to the instrument shop. And we could go along too!

We got to Liverpool in three hours that Saturday morning, with us Freezies in the back of Leo's dad's car, and Leo's dad and my dad up front. Round about noon we saw Mr Christaki coming along the road with his violin case. Miriam was holding his hand. We were waiting in the car outside the shop.

I was the one chosen to walk over to him.

"Hi, Mr Christaki," I said. "Are you all right?"

Mr Christaki looked startled. He started to turn and run, but Leo's dad got out of the car and stopped him. Leo and Sully got out too.

"We tracked you through the viola," Sully said.

"We'll help you fight to stay in the country," I piped in.

"And little Miriam too," Leo said.

Miriam looked frightened.

"You'll soon come home, darling," Leo's dad said to her.

"We must go," Mr Christaki said, turning to walk away.

But Leo's dad stopped him again. "If we found you, then the police will too. I'm a lawyer, and I think your chances for asylum are good. It's your decision."

Mr C was thinking.

"I have to be sure, Greg, about what I am to do now. My mind is in confusion for the first time. But thanks for all this. I must think."

Leo's dad nodded. Of course Mr C had to think. "Please give yourself up and claim asylum," he said, handing Mr C his card with his firm's phone number.

We left them there, saying goodbye with hugs all around.

At break on Monday, we were in the field behind the school parking lot when Leo said to Sully, "Why don't your mum and dad come to the committee meetings about Mr C and Miriam. Don't they want to save Mr C?"

Sully went all silent.

That evening at dinner, Mum asked me if Sully was all right.

"Why wouldn't she be all right?" I asked.

"They closed the post office in the village. Probably due to the fuss the *Salton Weekly* was making, calling it a waste of money to keep it open when Salton is just a few miles away. And now Sully's dad has lost his job."

"That's terrible."

"And, to make matters worse, her dad had a bust up with the newspaper people, threatening them and all. They wrote it up in the paper."

"Sully never said a thing about it," I said.

"Now her mum has to work in a cleaning plant or someplace like that."

So that's what had been bothering Sully.

# 12
## LEO'S TALE
# THE BLUNDER

**W**eeks went by. Katrina came back from Croatia and started doing all the stuff she used to do, taking Gabby to school and doing the cleaning. My dad didn't hear anything from Mr C, although we were all hoping he would ring him.

Everyone in Salton knew about Mr C. The *Salton Weekly* had made a big thing of it, saying that he had entered the country illegally and duped all the people of Jolyton and that the authorities were trying to find out if he had any connection to ISIS (that's a wicked terrorist group).

"The newspaper can be sued for that," Dad said. "It's outrageous nonsense!"

A picture of him appeared one day in the paper, with a caption that accused him of smuggling a child. One article said: "He took the good folk of Jolyton for a ride with a fiddle like the Pied Piper of Hamlyn."

Dad said whoever wrote that was an idiot because every child knows the Pied Piper played the flute and not the violin.

* * *

No one knew for sure what led to Mr C being arrested. We heard about it from Inspector Grey, who came to tell my dad the news.

"I am sorry to say we've got your Mr Christaki, sir. But maybe now with your assistance he'll be able to apply for asylum and stay in the country. I know that people round here, the community, want him to stay. But that's not up to us. I'll even say we've never had any trouble from him, if it helps."

"How did you find him?" I asked.

"We can't say, sir."

"What about the little girl?" I asked the officer.

"She's with Social Services in London, and they will want to know of any families willing to be interviewed for foster care while they find out exactly who she is and how Mr C got her here."

"There'll be twenty families willing to keep little Miriam," Dad reassured him. "But there's no need to look further—we would be very happy to keep her ourselves. She knows us and will be comfortable here. Poor little thing must be desperately frightened."

The Social Services people came and talked to my dad and mum, and the same day they drove Gabriella and Suleikha to London because Miriam knew them both well.

Then she came to us to stay. Mum even made up the spare room for her.

"Can't we speak to the government about Mr C?" I asked Dad. "Can't you?"

"Governments don't talk to people," Dad said.

I thought what Mr Christaki was going through was the worst thing that could happen to anyone, like someone you know half-dying. Except there's nothing anyone can do about someone dying—and here was a man being locked up who hadn't done anything wrong.

Now that Miriam was with us, she seemed happy playing with Gabby. Katrina helped with the little girl, but Gabby was now very determined to be "elder sister" and took charge of her from the time she woke up to when she came back from school. She even tried to boss Katrina around and change the times Katrina took Miriam out so she could go with them.

Gordon and Dad were working hard almost all the time on Mr Christaki's case, and Mum was going to Dad's office to discuss what she would say to a tribunal. Mr C was being kept in a place behind a high wire fence outside London, and they all three went to see him.

Mum got really furious when the *Salton Weekly* headlined what it called THE CHILLING CHRISTAKI STORY. Its account of the arrest sounded as though the worst terrorist in the world had been captured or as though aliens landing to invade and conquer had been nabbed. The reporter had spoken to officers from Liverpool who had arrested Mr Christaki and stressed that police and other agencies had very many ways of tracking down illegal immigrants.

Miss Honey told Mum, "We miss him so much at school—the children do." As if! She didn't miss him in school, she missed him in her heart. She was stuck on him. She even wrote to the *Salton Weekly* to say that "The community in Jolyton-cum-Barclay was grateful for Mr Christaki's work with children and for his cheerful and artistic presence in the village." Her letter said the paper should wait for evidence in the legal case and not "prejudge matters." The letter was published, and when we said "Three cheers for Miss Honey!" in class, she went red.

"I've told my dad I'm going to see Mr C if they go to the place again. Like not taking no for an answer," I told Kai.

"Me too then, if they allow kids," Kai said.

And soon after that it happened. A visit was planned and my dad said I could go. Mum said only if I did my homework, so I polished it off and we set sail.

"Can we take Miriam with us?"

"Sure," Dad said.

That's when we got the letter.

## 13

# A LETTER FROM MR C

*ear Greg, Gordon, members of the Committee formed to assist me and my Miriam, and also Leo, Suleikha and Kai,*

*I am so grateful to hear that Miriam is with Greg and Lucy's family and kindly looked after. You have taken care of my chief worry. I spend my time in this detention centre knowing that I do not deserve your attention, let alone your kindness in any special way.*

*I am writing this to explain why it was necessary to tell you all a lie. You have always been my friends and supporters, and it was very difficult for me not to tell you the truth. But there are reasons, which I beg you to please consider.*

*In my eyes I am not a criminal. I do not live with a guilty conscience, but I do not expect everyone to make the same judgement when they know the facts. All I want to do here is to put the facts plainly before you. I have been unfair to you. I am still the person whose acquaintance you made and whom you trusted with your children. I will understand perfectly if,* after reading this, you do not want to help me. I ask only that you read to the end.

Let me start at the beginning. I am an illegal immigrant, a refugee with a false Cypriot passport. I am actually Syrian, born and brought up in the north. My name is not Christaki. I was orphaned when I was six years old and brought up by Greek Orthodox missionaries in Aleppo, in Syria. The priests never attempted to convert me from the religion of my parents, which is Islam. They taught me Greek and English, Sophocles and Shakespeare. They also taught me mathematics and music—my favourite.

As a grown man working as a music teacher with the children in the Greek orphanage, the tragedy struck. The country was torn apart by the horrible war. A group called ISIS joined the war. You must have read about them. They were fanatics who killed and made slaves of people they didn't like. When their armies were on the border of our town, the priests, along with our whole community, said we had to run. We took every car and motorcycle and truck, and two hundred or more of us left for Turkey, whose border was quite close.

The ISIS people were everywhere on the road and we had to break through their checkpoints while they fired on us. I was with my childhood friend with whom I grew up in the orphanage. She was called Khadija and she had this little baby called Miriam. As we drove toward the Turkish border, Khadija was hit by a bullet in the head and died. I took charge of Miriam. We were taken by the Turkish army escort when we crossed the border, and most of the refugees were put in camps. But because we were with the Greek Christian priests, they put us on boats to Cyprus, where our priest protectors had connections. Father Suppolini assured us that we would be safe there, and we were.

In Cyprus, Father Suppolini testified that I was their adopted son and got me a passport with the name Georgiou Christaki. Of course it's not my real name. My real name is Suleiman Samaan. The funny thing is that at the orphanage everyone called me Sul, or Sully—and everytime I heard our own Suleikha called that I smiled inside myself.

I could have gone to Greece, but they are suspicious of people coming from Cyprus and claiming to be Greek. And they can tell that I am not, so because I speak English, I decided to make my way to the UK.

The fathers said they would look after Miriam, but I had grown up with Khadija, she was like my sister, so I told them I would come back for the child when I was settled.

I came here illegally, landing on a remote beach in Scotland by paying a Scottish fishing boat to bring me here.

And so when I was with you all, I began to see myself as Christaki, a name I was comfortable with. The lie became a truth in living it. And I felt so comfortable in your kindness. The fathers then sent Miriam to London with an English couple whom they paid. From there I brought her to Jolyton, as you all know. I admit I was foolish and thought I would never be caught, but life is not like that.

So this is where I am. I don't know what they will do with me. I thank you and God that Miriam will stay and perhaps be adopted by you. I beg you to.

*I thank you again for all your care and help. Whatever happens to me, it is my own fault.*

*Love to all,*

*Suleiman*

## 14

## SULLY'S TALE CONTINUES
# LIES AS TRUTH

My dad didn't always work for the post office. He used to be a journalist in Sri Lanka, where he came from. He had to leave Sri Lanka because he was being threatened by the government for writing stuff that opposed their views. So he was a refugee just like Mr C. Mum was a journalist too. That's how they met. In Jaffna, in Sri Lanka. He couldn't get a job as a journalist in England, but the post office hired him and sent him to Jolyton, our village. Mum did some part-time work here for an Indian news service but had to work at the supermarket too.

After I found out Dad had lost his job, I didn't feel like socializing with the Freezies as much. I was kind of depressed, I guess. To Leo and Kai, I know it felt like the triad was missing a leg.

That's when I started to visit Miss Barr. I think Miss Barr was lonely. Stranger things were to come.

If I was at her place and it got late, she would give me supper and I would stay the evening to finish my homework. Then she would phone to see if Mum or Dad were back and if they were, she'd drive me home, not up the lane, which was closed to cars, but all the way round the Mead and behind the hill. Her dogs, Porridge and Pudding, didn't scare me anymore. They just looked bad if you didn't know them, and that's what I began to think of Callista too. She used to offer them treats and even lumps of butter to eat and lick out of her hand. I thought that was disgusting at first but then she told me to feed them. They'd wolf up the treats without chewing and then start ticklishly licking my palm to mop up the crumbs and the taste.

When Dad got friendly with her and started asking her to pick me up from school because he couldn't, people began to notice. Then, one Monday in school, Leo said he and Kai had been to see Mr C in some prison-like camp. I felt bad about that. Because if we weren't friends like before, it was because at the back of my mind I was kinda confused.

Leo's mum had told us three that she was investigating legal ways to adopt Miriam, if she and the committee didn't succeed in getting Mr C back to Jolyton. And she told Mr C that she could apply for asylum so he could stay in the UK, but that he would have to answer a lot of questions truthfully about his past. Did she believe everything he had said in the letter? I actually asked her when she was telling us about all this. She answered, "My darling Suleikha, lawyers don't have to believe everything they are told. Clients sometimes don't tell their own lawyers everything."

"Like murderers," Leo had said.

\*\*\*

Gordon and Greg went to London when Mr C's case was set to start at a tribunal. Lucy was already in London and was the person who spoke to the authorities. When they all came back, the committee gathered at Kai's house. The three of them looked very serious. We were waiting outside in the garden, but this time Gordon said we could come in and listen. He spoke to a hushed room about what happened at the tribunal.

Mr C was threatened with being deported to Syria. He was accused of smuggling Miriam illegally into the country and withholding the names and contacts of the couple who had smuggled her in. He was also accused of travelling on a forged passport.

Greg said that only the Home Secretary, who was known for sending back anyone who had done anything wrong, could sign a paper to let him stay. And Mr Christaki had done several things wrong.

No date had been set for the deportation business to proceed.

"Can't you help him?" Leo asked his mum. "Dad always says you are high-flying."

"It's not me," Lucy said. "No one high up in government or the press who could tell the story to the public is interested in Mr Christaki. There are a few thousand people awaiting deportation. Why would anyone care about one individual who came to the UK illegally?"

"You mean Mr Christaki's name hasn't come up on the telly?" Leo asked.

"Yes, that's one way of putting it. Your Mr Christaki is not a celebrity. If he were a football player instead of a music teacher and antique fixer in a village, it might be different. There'd be newspapers and TV, and then there'd be votes on it. That's what the government cares about—votes!"

"Then why don't you get Miriam and Mr C put on TV?" Leo asked. But of course he knew the answer. Just anyone couldn't go on TV.

But then Leo had this great idea.

"We should play as a group in Salton Town Square—as The Christaki Trio, even if that sounds a bit classical—and if the newspapers see us, we can say that Mr Christaki is a very good music teacher and is being thrown out of the country. At least we'll get some attention."

I agreed with that of course, but I also wanted us to be together as a trio again. And when Leo said, "Like the old days, Sully," I pretended I didn't know what he meant.

This would be The Christaki Trio's first public appearance. We started practising some songs together at Leo's house. We had a lot of pieces we played as duets, and since we couldn't take a piano into the market square, Leo had to borrow a keyboard, which Miss Honey said he could have from school. But it worked on electricity so we would have to ask one of the shops that Kai's dad was friendly with to plug it in.

It was while making the arrangements for our little concert that we found out that Miss Honey used to go to the illegal immigrants' detention centre to see Mr C on her own. One day she let her secret slip when she said, "I'll tell Suleiman what you children are doing. He'll be pleased."

"So it's Suleiman now, is it?" Kai said aloud but not to her. How cheeky or intimate is that? But she saw us staring and I could swear she blushed.

Leo and Kai made up a song about it all:

*Think of a man*
*Far from home*
*Or a child that's on the run*
*You say it's nothing to do with you*
*But it's something you have done*

*Birds fly where they want*
*Their ceiling is the sky*
*But men are owned by countries*
*No one can tell us why.*

*Think of lonely*
*People who*
*Are forced to run away*
*From poverty, hunger, cruelty*
*The dark clouds of the day.*

It had a very sad tune. Leo was going to sing it and we'd do the chorus and then add bits on the instruments. Gordon said he would phone the other parents and they could even sponsor us. I said he shouldn't phone my dad, because he wasn't in town.

Leo made up a big placard, saying:

## THE CHRISTAKI TRIO
### CLASSICAL AND POP REQUESTS WELCOME
### BRING BACK MR CHRISTAKI
### BRING BACK THE MUSIC

Greg drove us to Salton Town Square. The market was on and stalls were set up. We found a corner where the pavement was curved outside a bank, which was closed that day, and next to it was the Oxfam shop where we had permission to plug in the keyboard. Leo had brought his cousin's karaoke amplifier to make our music louder.

We put him in charge because he's not shy and quite bossy. I felt kind of nervous and embarrassed, but this was what we had decided to do, so we had to do it. I put my flute to my mouth and began, and then Kai joined me, and soon five or six people had gathered to listen and they were smiling. We were playing a piece called "Etude," which Mr C made us play over and over again. As we finished, a man and an old lady threw some change onto Kai's keyboard cover.

"No, thank you," Leo said, "we're not doing it for money. Please read the banner."

"Who is Mr Christaki?" the man asked.

Kai held out the clipboard on which we had several sheets of paper that Kai's dad had printed out. It was a petition that people could write their names on and sign. It read:

> *We the undersigned wish to demonstrate our concern for Georgiou Christaki and the four-year-old Miriam Christaki, who are to be deported from the UK to Syria.*
>
> *We ask that the Home Office reconsider the decision and let Mr Christaki and Miriam, who have made a home in Jolyton-Cum-Barclay, remain as useful and valued members of the community.*

The man signed and then four other people also signed and Kai and Leo began to play some music to thank them. More people came and signed. Some of them asked for more information about Mr Christaki and Miriam, and we told them he was our music teacher and that our parents were helping him. Then I played the song of "The Jolly Miller" on my own, and after that we sang our new song. The crowd that had gathered clapped, and the news spread all round the market place.

By the afternoon, we had filled ten sheets of the petition and Leo's dad took us back to Jolyton. We gave him the petition, which he looked over, saying, "You are very brave. A hundred and twenty people heard you play. Well done. Celebrity at last."

The next day we appeared in the *Salton Weekly*. It had a picture of us playing on the steps of the bank, but what it said was: "The people of Salton should not encourage metropolitan habits like begging in our public places." It said that the town council should come down hard on busking in the streets.

"This is disgusting," Leo's dad said to us. He was very angry, because he had called the paper and told them we would be playing in the square. He said he was "hopping" and was going to drive to Salton to wring the editor's neck. He used the F-word and a couple of B-words and had to be calmed down by Leo's mum.

At school we got lots of kids and parents and teachers to sign the petition, and even the headmistress signed. Kai's dad sent off the petition to someone in London. It had over 600 signatures. He received a reply saying: "We have noted your efforts."

We were getting desperate. We needed another idea, and

this time Kai came up with it. "Do you remember *The Diary of Anne Frank*?"

Of course I'd seen the film about this girl who hides from the Nazis in Amsterdam so they can't take her family to a camp for Jews and kill them.

"Mr Christaki said he wrote a diary and I think it's in the house in his desk. It may be something like that, and if we send it to someone and they make it into a real book, he might get famous and then he won't be sent back," Kai said.

We thought it was worth a try. That evening we again took down the board that we had propped up over the back door and entered Water Meadow House. We opened all the drawers and looked everywhere for the diary. We found a book in which he had written in some strange script. Inside was an envelope with some money.

We decided to give it to Mr C. He could use it in the detention centre to buy stuff he needs.

## 15

## SULLY'S STRATAGEM

# A LIE MAY ASSIST THE TRUTH

One day when I was playing a flute duet with Callista, her phone rang. She said, "Your dad," but I couldn't hear what they said to each other. Then Mum came on the phone. I could hear her voice, and Miss Barr said to her, "I couldn't think of anything better. If Suleikha would like that though."

"That was Mum," I said.

"Yes it was, and you know what? They are going to talk to you and, if you agree, you are going to spend a whole week or more with me. I shall take you to school and back, and we can eat what you like and have your friends over and think of nice things to do. I am going to play fairy godmother."

"Really? But why?" I asked.

"Surprise. Maybe more good news. Let them tell you."

"Mum's not having another baby, is she?" I asked.

Miss Barr laughed. "No, no, no, no. Silly child."

Dad and Mum were waiting when Callista dropped me at home.

"We have to tell you what's going on," Dad said.

"And ask your permission," Mum said. "Callista's given you a posh tea, I suppose?"

"Salmon and asparagus," I said.

"Humph," Dad said.

"Miss Barr told me that you're going forever to Australia and that she's adopting me," I said, sitting down on the settee.

Mum looked puzzled till Dad said, "Nice one, Sully."

Then Mum hugged me. "Darling, Dad and I have decided that we are going to look for a job managing and running a pub," she said.

"A pub?"

"Yes," Dad said. "We have to go to interviews with three different breweries. They wanted couples, so I applied and answered questions, and now they want to meet and ask us more things. Then if they like us and think we are suitable, they can send us anywhere in the country. It could be north, south, east, west, city, town or village. It would be a new start."

I was shocked. "Then we'd have to leave Jolyton and . . . school and my best friends," I said.

"Yes, I know," Mum said. She was sitting next to me on the settee, looking serious. She put her hands gently on my shoulders.

"We have to make a living," Dad said. "I don't want to leave, but Jolyton is too small to find a new job. It'll be hard work, but with Mum's cooking we can make a go of it."

"We might be lucky and get a pub near here," Mum said. "Then you could see your friends."

"There's only The Hotty here," I said.

"Might be London and all the shops. You'll make new friends."

Parents don't know how hard it is to make friends and keep

them. They just talk rubbish.

"I don't want new friends, thanks," I said.

"What it means," Mum said, "is that we have to go away on Sunday for about ten days. And we could have asked granny to come and stay, but she's been ill. We could have asked Leo's dad and mum, and they would have gladly kept you for a week. But they have Miriam now."

"So your mum suggested asking Miss Barr. She thought you'd be very happy spending some days with her. It turns out Miss Barr thinks we are doing her a favour, lending her our Sully for a week."

"Is that okay?" Mum asked.

"Whatever," I said.

When I saw her anxious look, I knew I was being mean. "I just said that for fun. Miss Barr is great and I'll have a cool time. It will be like a holiday. I hope you and Dad get a pub and a job. Okay?"

Mum hugged me. "Are you sure? We'll give Miss Barr a key, so if you get homesick or I've forgotten to pack something, you can get it from the house. A whole ten days! What'll I do, Sully-mully?" Mum said.

"You'll survive," I said.

Mum called Miss Barr and started giving her instructions. "She loves eating whatever you give her. Please don't go out of your way." As if I was a pet or something.

On Sunday morning they dropped me off at Miss Barr's with my suitcase full of clothes, books and my paints and things.

"We'll have a whale of a time, and we'll call you every day," Miss Barr said to them.

It was when I was sitting by the river on the other side, staring at Mr C's empty house, that some little thought, some beginning of a plan, came to me. It kept going round in my head, and when I thought about it more, I knew I still hadn't thought it through.

I couldn't tell Callista that I was trying to work out a plan. It was not something adults would approve of, and she might even stop me. She'd made a delicious tea, and we turned on the telly to a program about a baby polar bear who gets separated from its mum and gets stuck in the middle of the ocean on an ice floe.

"Poor bear, home alone," Callista said.

That was it! Settled. Finally I had a plan, perfectly formed.

It was like she had read my thoughts. How weird is that! I hadn't given my thoughts a name, but it came to me when she said that. I was sure the plan would work, though it could go badly—a big lie for a big truth.

I didn't see Leo and Kai that evening. I thought of phoning them, I was that excited about my plan, but didn't want Callista to overhear, so I left it.

My bedroom overlooked the river, and I could see Miriam's room on the top floor and the big picture window, dark and reflecting the moon. I drew the curtains then got into bed. The thought of putting the plan into action gave me a sinking feeling in my tum.

In the morning, Callista knocked on the door and said, "Wakeys! Brush your teeth and down to breakfast. School time soon." No, I couldn't tell her. As I said, adults, however friendly, don't understand these things. Kai and Leo would.

I waited to tell them till it was nearly home time.

"I thought of a way to get me on the telly," I said. "So I can draw everyone's attention to Miriam and Mr Christaki," I said.

"Okay," Leo said. "What's this master plan?"

I told them.

"But your dad and mum will look bad," Leo said.

He was right. My dad and mum would be publicly shamed. They had done nothing wrong. They would never forgive me. But there was no choice. A higher purpose like in that book *A Tale of Two Cities*.

"We've got six days then. Get a move on!" Kai said.

The next day I told Callista that she didn't need to pick me up from school as I was invited to Leo's. I knew she wouldn't ask any questions. I made up similar excuses for the next three days so as to avoid any adult dropping me at school or picking me up. Then I told her I had to get to Leo's early on Tuesdays and Wednesdays because we did extra maths with his dad before school. That all meant I walked alone to and from school for several days. Leo and Kai helped by pretending to their dads and mums that there was some secret about me they weren't telling. They'd shout, "Oh there's Sully, all by herself!" or something like that, so their parents would notice.

On the third day, Greg stopped to give me a lift because he and Leo saw me at the bottom of our lane a little way from their gate. I climbed into their car and went with them to school. And that evening Leo and I stood and waited till his mum came to pick him up and, as I started walking away, she called out to me.

"Where are you walking to, Sully?"

"Home," I said.

"Get in then, we'll take you," she said.

I took the lift.

"Your dad will be there, will he?" she asked.

"Yes, Dad and Mum." I had to lie. Our plan was working.

I got out and let myself into our house with my key. Then, leaving all the lights on, I ran down the hill to Water Meadow Lane and crossed the bridge to Callista's.

"Did it go okay?" she asked. "I've got a piping hot fish pie for you."

In the evenings, Mum and Dad would phone Callista, and I would speak to them. "How did the interviews go?" All that stuff. Mum only wanted to say wet stuff like she was missing me, and Dad was boasting about how he had impressed the bosses. They had been in London and then drove to Wales, where they'd be for some days. They said they didn't know how long.

"We are doing fine," Callista said.

"Mum, can I go to Kai's on Saturday for his birthday? There's a sleepover and Callista wanted me to ask you. It's safe and all, yeah?"

"It's not up to me. It's for Callista to say. She can say yes or no, and then that's that."

Callista said, "Of course you must go."

"A few more days, darling," Mum said.

Callista would pack lunch in the mornings. She was a health nut—brown bread sandwiches with hummus and salmon and fancy stinky cheese and funny pointy tomatoes, yogurt, plums and bananas and things that Mum would never get. At lunchtime, I didn't go into the dining hall where packed-lunchers ate.

I gobbled my lunch behind the car park.

"Why weren't you in the dining hall at lunch?" Miss Honey asked me.

"Don't feel hungry today, Miss," I said and made a sort of sick face. She may be a drama teacher, but she didn't know that I was acting.

The next day I ate my lunch behind the buildings near the bike shed where Jason and gang used to go to smoke their dope. On Friday I was out in the playground at lunchtime when Miss Honey came up to me.

"No lunch?"

"No, Miss," I said.

"Weren't you packed a lunch?"

"She hasn't got any," Kai said.

"I don't understand," said Miss Honey.

I just looked away and started walking off.

She came after me. "What's the matter, Sully?"

But then she got distracted by Jason and some of the boys climbing on the roof of the mobile classroom in the corner of the playground to get a ball, and she rushed off to stop them.

Miss Honey was a big part of the plan.

The evening before, we had all gathered at Callista's. Leo played the piano and we kept talking about Kai's birthday and sleepover on Saturday. Of course, you might have guessed the truth. It wasn't Kai's birthday and there was no sleepover. That too was to throw Callista off the trail, but onto the trail, as you'll see. Our lie would become her truth.

"We must get Kai a present," she said, and on Saturday morning she drove me to Bimbury to buy it. We got him a book, what else. I felt terrible, because Callista was buying wrapping paper and a card and everything. But plans are plans.

Callista said I should wear something nice for the party—a dress? "Nah, jeans and sweater," I said. "I'll probs be the only girl there except for his cousin." I packed my pyjamas and tooth-brush in a denim bag and carried the wrapped-up present. She dropped me at Kai's gate and, as we'd arranged, Kai came to greet me. We waited till Callista turned the car round, waved, and then Kai and I walked up the hill to my house. We watched a bit of telly and the two of us roughed up the kitchen a bit and then Kai went home. I waited alone. I didn't like it, but I did it.

At ten o'clock, three hours after Kai left, I heard a car outside. The bell rang. It was Miss Honey. I answered it. I was expecting her but pretended to be surprised.

"Are your parents here, Sully?" she asked.

I didn't answer.

"Have your parents left you alone? My God, Sully, are you all right?"

I tried to look sad and tired. "Who told you?"

"Leo did. You poor child. I thought there was something odd. How long have they been gone?"

Again I didn't reply, but she came in and started looking round.

"Where are your parents?"

"I don't know, Miss."

She looked disturbed. "How can you not know?" she asked. "How long, Suleikha?"

"Two, three weeks."

"Weeks! Why didn't you tell someone? Where have they gone?"

"I don't know, they just went. I think they went on a holiday."

"They did no such thing. I know your parents. My God. Where's your phone? I'm not carrying mine."

"I don't think they meant to like . . . you know . . . leave me . . . but . . ."

She held her hand out and I gave her my phone.

"I know. They would never do that. Something has happened to them. My God, I hope they are okay. This doesn't sound at all right." She began to call.

Things were going according to plan.

Leo and Kai had made me rehearse my answers. Miss Honey didn't ask about money, but we had planned what I should say about it, so I blurted it out.

"I can't find any money in the house, and my dad and mum don't have mobile phones, so I couldn't call them," I said.

"Suleikha, this is serious! I don't know what to say. This is very serious. Do you realize that?" Miss Honey almost shouted. "I mean, where would they have gone? It's illegal. Why didn't you tell me? Did they tell you they were going? You should have told us or even the damn police, for God's sake!"

"No, they just disppeared. They didn't leave a note or nothing."

I turned my face away. I didn't want her to look into my eyes. I felt sick. And that same sinking feeling in my stomach, which happens when things go wrong. But this time it was happening because things were going exactly as we wanted them to. I knew that everyone except Kai and Leo would be angry with me. People would never forgive me. Especially not Mum and Dad for saying wicked things about them.

Miss Honey did what Leo said she'd do. She took my phone, called the police and reported that I was home alone and only twelve years old, even though I was nearly thirteen. She said something may have happened to my mum and dad and then she went into the kitchen to see if I had any food there. Mum had cleared out the fridge before they left.

A little while later, Inspector Grey and a lady in a suit called at the house. Miss Honey said I should talk to them. They asked me questions and I mostly said I didn't know. I said all I knew was that Mum and Dad had gone away and I didn't know where they were.

I told them Dad was desperate because he didn't have a job, and he was looking for one. They went upstairs and poked about. The lady said she was a social worker and that Miss Honey could take me to her place. Just as we stepped out, even though it was night, we saw a bus and a car on the road and three people on the drive. Two of them started taking photographs of me and Miss Honey with their flashing cameras.

Leo and Kai had called the papers.

More policemen arrived and one held the reporter and the camera people back while we walked to Miss Honey's car. One reporter started shouting questions.

Callista didn't know anything about any of this. Yet. I called her later and said Miss Honey was taking some of us to a play, so Miss Honey said I could stay at her place. Callista said she was happy with that if I was.

\*\*\*

The next morning I rode to school with Miss Honey. Some parents had read the story in the newspaper, and a couple of girls and Jason came up to me in the playground at break and asked about it. Miss Honey saw them and immediately spirited me away and took me to the libary. She said I should spend the day reading on my own. The library would be out of bounds for the rest of the kids that day.

Miss Honey said I was now going to stay with her and should get my things from my house, so when school ended she came to pick me up from the library. As we walked out, Miss Chapman came up to us. She looked a bit frantic.

"There's a couple of reporters and TV people outside, and the kids are going wild. Mrs Husky has called the police."

All according to plan.

"I can walk home with Kai," I said.

"Don't be silly," Miss Honey said. "You're going with me in the car."

Driving out of the gates we saw two TV camera crews and a reporter from a London paper. Miss Honey blew the horn as the reporter came up to us and I could hear my name being shouted. The kids were crowding around the gates and crews even though some teachers were trying to disperse them. The car couldn't get through.

And then I did it. But first I closed my eyes tight till they hurt, then opened them again, because I had never done anything like this before, and I promise I never will again. I got out of Miss Honey's car, and as loudly as I could, said, "I am the home alone girl. I want to say something."

Immediately a young lady and another man with a camera

pushed through the crowd of kids, which had gone deadly quiet, as though they were waiting for me to say something. The man with the camera said, "Sunita, what do you think happened to your mum and dad?" He got my name wrong.

"What have you been eating?" the lady asked.

"Weren't you scared at night?" the reporter shouted.

"I want to say something," I said again and again.

Eventually all went silent.

"See, my parents wouldn't leave me alone. They are not like that. So something has happened to them, and you know what? The day my dad and mum—like went missing—they had gone to see a person called Mr Christaki, and he also disappeared the same day. But I think the police got him and he is in a detention place. If the TV, papers and police want to know why I am home alone, then you've got to find out why Mr Christaki, the best music teacher in the world, disappeared the same day as my mum and dad and why he is being sent away from this country. My mum and dad went to see Mr Christaki and they all disappeared from the village together. And that's all."

Miss Honey stepped out to get me back into the car, but she was listening.

The silence hung in the air for a few more seconds, and then they started shouting questions.

"What are you talking about, Sully?"

"Where did they go?"

Miss Honey had a startled look on her face. Suddenly she understood.

"Mr Christaki was our music teacher. That's all I know." My voice came out much softer than I thought it would. And it was like I wasn't speaking the words that were coming out of my mouth. I was somewhere far away from them.

Miss Honey looked at me. She shook her head in wonder.

It was working. The TV cameras were there and they'd taken down what I said.

Miss Honey held me by the shoulders, quite kindly, and looked into my face. Her eyes were wet. Then she hurried me toward the car and bundled me in. As we moved off, she wound the window down and shouted, "That's all she wants to say. Find Mr Christaki in the detention centre. He has an immigration appeal going."

We got to her house and shut the door and she made us both some hot chocolate.

She kept saying "Oh my God!"

# 16

## MORE SULLY

# THE FEDORA'S PLAN

The doorbell rang and Miss Honey answered it. I heard a woman's voice saying she knew that the home alone girl, Suleikha, was there and could she speak to me. At least this one got my name right.

Miss Honey brought a young lady into the room. She was pretty, I thought, and wearing a man's hat.

"Suleikha, this is Joanna from the regional BBC news. She'd like to speak to you. I am sure you'd like to speak to her."

She invited Joanna to sit.

"I think I know what you're after, Suleikha," Joanna said, sitting down. "This Mr Christaki, we've found out which detention centre he's in. What do you think we should ask him?" She took off her hat and spun it like a top onto the carpet next to her, which I thought was odd.

"Just put him on the telly," I said.

"There has to be a reason for someone to appear on TV. I have to have a reason for taking a TV crew to him."

Miss Honey came back into the room with coffee and biscuits.

"He's an amazing person, and the village needs him to stay. Besides, he'll be killed if he is sent back to Syria. And there's Miriam."

"Miriam?" she asked.

That's when I told her the whole story about Mr Christaki, Miriam, the music lessons, Miss Barr, Water Meadow House, the people who wanted Mr C gone from the village . . . well, everything that you know up to now. I told Joanna the whole thing. And she had it on her mobile phone.

After I finished, she got up and left the room. A few minutes later, she came back talking on her phone.

"I spoke to my editor and we have found your Mr Christaki. He is at Napier Barracks in Kent. So what do you suggest we ask him?"

"Is that the detention centre some inmates set fire to, because it's so dreadful?"

"Yes, they were complaining about being locked in because of shortage of staff, and about the time it was taking for their claims to be processed—months, even years."

"Mr Christaki wouldn't have started fires," I said. "He's not like that."

"No, no that was long before he got there," Joanna said.

Her phone rang then, and she got up again to take the call. She paced about, walking into other rooms as though it was her own house.

"Fantastic . . . yes, I'm sure they will . . . I'm with them now . . . yes, one of the teachers. Right . . . yeah. Great . . . bye!"

Joanna came back into the room looking excited. She didn't bother to sit down.

"How many pupils did your Christaki do music with?"

"From our school? Maybe twelve?"

"But he wrote music for our play, and that was with fifty," Miss Honey said.

"Here's what Tom, my editor, said. He called the local MP and the immigration officer in charge of Napier Barracks," she said. "Ever since the fire there, they've had a problem with their PR."

"PR?" I asked.

"Their public relations, what people think of the place," Miss Honey said.

"Do you teach music, Miss Honey?" Joanna asked.

"Please, it's Aurelia—just Lia will do. And yes, I deal with some music, but I'm the drama department all on my own."

"Tom said he'll put together an item about Mr Christaki teaching music that will show him in a brilliant light. It'll be a real scoop. How about tomorrow?"

I felt like jumping up and down. My home alone trick had done its job, which was to get Mr C's story on TV. It was all a lie, but might lead to the truth about Mr Christaki and Miriam.

And so Joanna and a TV crew arrived at the school and interviewed staff and kids and even parents picking up their kids. All the adults had to sign what they called release forms.

Joanna interviewed Mr Christaki at the detention centre. She still wore a man's hat. Leo said it was called a fedora and that his grandad used to wear one.

Joanna's report about my "home alone silliness" and Mr Christaki's detention and music teaching at the school were on the telly that evening. They said an interview with him would air the next day. Miss Barr saw it on TV and realized that I had been telling her a lot of lies.

I said to her, "You probably want to throw me out now." But no. She just reached over and gave me a big hug. So I told her the whole story, everything I had done. She sat down and listened very quietly and nodded. It was like she understood why we had made up this plan, why I had lied to her. I said I was sorry. She held my hand in both of hers. I had expected her to be angry. But she wasn't angry.

The next day after school, Miss Honey said she'd fetch Kai and Leo so we could watch the interview together. I started breathing deeply as though I'd been running a marathon.

"It's the relief," she said. "Take deep breaths."

When Miss Honey arrived with Kai and Leo at Miss Barr's house, Kai's parents drove up too. Leo's parents joined us soon after. They brought Katrina and Gabby and Miriam and Jumper. We were all going to watch the interview with Mr C.

"But, Suleikha, you know that your dad and mum will be known all over the country as bad parents?" Leo's mum said as Callista welcomed them in.

"I knew that. It's the bad bit, the lie to get something true done," I said as I felt the panic in my guts.

"Don't worry. You've done it now," Kai's dad, the philosopher, said. "It's for a greater good."

"I'm sure your plan will be of help for Mr Christaki's case," Miss Barr said. "Fingers crossed." And then she became thoughtful. "Hmmm," she said, twisting her mouth, but didn't say what she was thinking.

We all sat down around the telly, and soon Mr Christaki was on. He was sitting at a table across from Joanna in an office at his prison. He told his whole story. He said he had come to the UK with a false passport, running from war, with Greek Christian priests, all running from certain death. He explained that Miriam was the daughter of a friend who had died by gun-fire, and that priests in Cyprus, who had been looking after her, brought her here. Joanna asked him if he had officially adopted her, and Mr Christaki said, "No, I had no time."

He looked tired but was speaking very confidently as though he didn't care what happened to him. Only when he mentioned Miriam did he look a bit sad. He pulled out his wallet and showed Joanna four or five photographs of her, and Joanna said, "Oh, she's an absolute darling! She is being well cared for back in the village where you lived, and with people with whom she is familiar. We saw her and spoke to her."

"Is she asking for me?"

"Yes, every two minutes."

Mr Christaki closed his eyes for a few seconds and then opened them again. "We escaped certain death."

Leo's dad said, "Getting this on TV will make the government think more carefully about it."

"Other papers from around the world have started phoning. So it's working, Sul," Kai's dad said.

Joanna gave the interview without mentioning anything about me being home alone, but the news hounds to whom I had shouted at the school gates had put two and two together.

"I am sure we will be able to move the case up to the tribunal quickly now," Lucy said.

Then Miss Honey turned to me. "The papers will be ruthless with your mother and father if they don't know that it was all a ploy." Panic gripped my guts again. She was right. I couldn't even think how angry Dad would be.

So Callista called them and left messages, because neither had answered, and we waited for Mum and Dad to call back.

Just as everyone was leaving, Callista said, "You know, I used to work at Channel 4 and in journalism. I can give some friends there and at the big dailies, *The Guardian* and *The Independent*, a call. It's only eight o'clock, and if they are going to follow up on the story, they might want to hear the truth."

The next day at school, Leo told me his mum had heard from the Home Office and that it had permitted an appeal to a special asylum tribunal that will be heard in the next day or two. Leo's mum would argue the case at the tribunal. She said a strong case could be made for Mr C's forged passport, because the European Court ruled that using a forged passport to escape death or imprisonment was not considered illegal. I hadn't slept much, expecting Mum and Dad to ring even in the middle of the night, but they didn't. Maybe they hadn't see the news in Wales. But by morning, if the newspapers had the story, they'd know and they'd come straight back.

Miss Barr had the *Salton Weekly* at the top of a pile of news-papers. It had lied, saying that Mum and Dad had been spotted in London on the big giant wheel called The London Eye. They were enjoying themselves miles away from their young daughter, who they left in Jolyton-cum-Barclay without food and money.

"Vicious stuff," Callista said as her phone rang. It was the police. They told her that I was not to speak to the press any more because a judge had ruled that they were wrong to publish my picture, and the papers may be in trouble. Some even had got my age wrong. They said I was eleven!

Six other papers had our story. All of them had pictures of Mr Christaki and a lot of stuff about Miriam. One newspaper wrote: HOME ALONE GIRL IN PLEA FOR MUSIC TEACHER AND LITTLE FRIEND. Another said: SULLY WANTS HER CHRISTAKI. They had pages about Mr Christaki and pictures of Aleppo and Raqqa and of the war in Syria. Then more stuff about the prison place he was in.

When my phone finally rang, I answered it to hear my dad shouting down it.

"What the hell is going on?"

"Tell your dad you are safe and then let me talk to him," Callista whispered.

"I'm sorry, Dad. I'm fine. Miss Barr will tell you what is going on." She took the phone out of my hand and spoke to him.

By the time I got back on the phone, Dad wasn't shouting. I could tell he was still really angry, but he managed to use a calm voice. "Why did you do this to us?"

"It was the only way I could help Mr Christaki."

"Do you know what you've done to your mother and me, Suleikha?" Then Mum was crying on the phone, but she said she was glad I was well and looked after. She said I should thank Callista for looking after me, and they were coming back immediately. They would pick me up from school that afternoon.

\*\*\*

Kai and Leo had walked down to Callista's house so we could walk to school together.

"The papers are mostly, like, taking your side," Kai said.

"I'm just thinking of Dad and Mum and what I've done to them," I answered.

Reporters were still at the gates, but Inspector Grey was also there to stop them from taking pictures of me.

The whole class started asking questions as soon as I got inside, but Kai and Leo kept them off. Everyone knew about what we'd done and why we'd done it.

"Interviews with Sully cost a fiver," Leo said.

I got called to Mrs Husky's office during the last lesson. Mum and Dad had arrived and were sitting there. Mum hugged me. Her eyes were red from crying.

"I'm sorry," I said.

Dad was quiet and didn't even look at me.

"I think you've got some explaining to do, Sully," Mrs Husky said. "You can do it right here, or you can go home with your mum and dad, who've been very unfairly treated."

"We'd best go home," Dad said.

On the way home he was very calm. Something I hadn't expected. "We think we know why you did it, Suleikha, and I want you to know that in your place I would have done the same," he said. "If you think some very bad and unjust things are being done and you make a plan to fight against them, then I support you."

I was shocked. It was as though this was someone else and not my dad at all. I was waiting for him to explode, to disown me. And then this?

As we got to the edge of the Mead, he stopped the car suddenly. I was sitting next to him in the front seat, and Mum was in the back. He gave me a big kiss and a big smile. "It's put us deep in the muck."

"Your dad missed his final interview today," Mum said. "But after what the papers said about us, even if he'd gone for the interview, they would have laughed in his face."

"I don't think I want to take over a pub anyway," Dad said. "I don't think I could do it, day in and day out, standing behind a bar pulling beer."

"I didn't think any of this would happen, Dad. It was to get Mr Christaki's case on TV. Nothing else. I knew it would hurt you, to tell the truth. I'm really sorry."

"I've already said, little one, that I support you. Mr Christaki, Suleiman, should fight the government, and that little girl should have a dad who cares for her, even if he isn't her dad. I read all the papers. I read them and thought my Sully is doing a serious thing. Then I stopped being angry."

"The *Salton Weekly* found out that the brewery people had taken us to The London Eye," Mum said with tears in her eyes, "and splashed that all over the paper."

"Did Miss Barr have anything to do with your plan?" Dad asked. "Tell me the truth, Sully."

"She didn't know anything about it," I said. "I told her some lies. It had nothing to do with her."

Dad nodded. "And your two pals helped, I suppose, phoning the police and papers? The *Salton Weekly* has it in for me. It ran that campaign to shut the post office."

\* \* \*

Our home phone was ringing as we walked through the door. Dad picked it up and Mum started opening the windows.

"That was Callista," Dad said. "She said she's going to London overnight."

When the doorbell rang just then, Mum answered it and we saw a policeman and a policewoman at the door. Out at the gate was a man with a camera.

"I'm from the *Salton Weekly*," we heard him say, "and I'd like to talk to you."

"I know where you're from, and I read your lying rubbish," Dad shouted. "Just push off."

The man started flashing pictures of Dad. Before Mum could stop him, Dad went wild, reached for the man's camera and flung it onto the road. The police officers sent him packing before Mum invited them into the house.

"It's all lies," I said to them when we got inside. "I made it all up. Dad and Mum left me with my godmother, and I was never alone."

The policeman listened carefully. He didn't miss a thing. "Is that what your dad told you to say?" he asked.

"No, that's the truth," I said.

"We must have a little chat, Sully," the lady officer said.

Mum told me to go upstairs to my room. A bit later the police went away, and Mum came up to tell me they would be back the next day to interview me.

After dinner I watched the evening news on TV. "The parents of the home alone twelve-year-old girl have returned and are being interviewed by the police," the newsman was saying. "But what the girl said to the press has set off a chain reaction."

The policewoman came back early the next morning. She advised me not to go to school because a lot of newspaper people were still hanging about. "Never seen anything like it in this village."

She said she had to talk to me and that Mum should be there. She asked Mum if she could record our conversation.

"Do what you like," Mum said. "We have nothing to hide."

We sat in the front room. I told her that it was all my idea. I didn't bring the others into it.

"Your plan has worked, but that's not the way to do things, Sully. Look at the trouble you've caused. For your mum and dad," she said, switching off the recording device she had brought. "I don't know if you're out of trouble, but you might get called in and told off for wasting police time."

"When things settle down, she'll get told off for more than just that," Mum said.

A letter arrived later that day from the brewery people telling Dad they didn't want him in any pub job. We took turns reading it. I couldn't even say sorry any more. That was worse than falsely blaming them for my home alone lies. I had taken Dad and Mum's earnings away. I felt like disappearing into a hole in the ground, if one would just open up, but it didn't.

After school the two other Freezies came to our house on their bikes.

"Our dads and Leo's mum have gone to London to see about Mr Christaki's appeal," Kai said. "Miss Honey's gone too."

"Ooooo!" Leo said.

Joanna, the BBC reporter, dropped in too and introduced

herself to my mum, adding that "Hundreds of people have phoned the BBC to say they'll adopt Miriam if Mr C gets sent away." She asked if I was willing for a follow-up story. I looked at Mum, and when she nodded, I said yes we could do that after Mr Christaki came back home. She said I should be a TV producer, because that was exactly the angle they would use.

The next day was Saturday and us Freezies biked down to Callista's place. But the house was locked, and her car and the dogs were gone. So we came back to my house. Mum made an Indian lunch for everyone.

When the phone rang, she answered it and I watched as her eyes lit up. "The appeal is over and Mr Christaki is allowed to stay in the country!" she said, beaming after hanging up. "That was Greg in London." She turned to Leo. "Your mum, Lucy, must have put together a fantastic case."

We were all stunned at first, and then we started jumping up and down and high-fiving and shouting "Yayyyyy!" with fists raised in the air and grabbing each other for hugs.

"You did it, Sully," said Leo.

"You should be our leader," Kai said.

"A tripod stands on its own," I said. "It doesn't need leaders."

Greg and Gordon brought Mr Christaki back with them from London. We were waiting at the gate of Water Meadow House, and we all cheered when they drove in. Miss Honey was following them. Katrina pulled up with Gabby and Miriam, who ran up to Mr C and started hugging him. She hugged each of us and gave us all kisses.

"I hope I get to keep Miriam," Mr C said, standing at the open door.

A fine mist was in the air as we said goodbye to him, and it looked like steam was coming off the river. All of a sudden the lights at Miss Barr's house and garden came on. The house looked like a big floating ship above the mist.

"Callista's back," I said.

"I saw her at the appeal. She came and went and didn't speak to anyone," Mr Christaki said.

Callista's dogs started barking, and we went over to see her.

"You did it, Sully. It worked. And no one got hurt."

"My dad was good about it," I said.

"Great and fabulous. Now let me tell you something about me. I'm fed up with living in this village and writing jewellery articles for the London fashion papers, so I'm going to get back into being a proper reporting newspaper woman."

"How?"

"When I went to London, I saw my ex-husband. The company he works for owns lots of newspapers, but they know that a lot of the future is online so they want to start a fresh web paper. I told him our story and he loved it."

"Are you going to marry him again?" I asked.

"Good God, no. He is happily married to someone else. But I'll tell you what I heard from him. The people who own the *Salton Weekly* asked him and his large newspaper company if they wanted to buy it. You see, it's losing money and has to fold. No more local newspaper. So no horrid stories."

"Do you mean fold, like closed down for good?" Leo asked.

"Yes, and they've asked me to edit the new web paper.

Something that will interest all sections of the entire community. Not local. National, but from here! So what shall we call it? The *Salton Triangle*, like the Bermuda Triangle, where all sorts of mysterious things happen?"

Kai and Leo said their dads told them that Callista and her ex-husband had been the ones who pushed some important ministers into sorting out the asylum for Mr C.

The next morning Callista came to our house. I thought Dad might say something to her about all that stuff, but she didn't give him a chance. "I am very sorry for not being more careful with her," she said. "It must have been upsetting and horrible for you. Still, all's well and swell."

"Lost me a job," Dad said.

"That's what I came to talk to you about. I'm going to be the editor of a new and nationally backed web newspaper. My ex is sponsoring it, and it has good financial backing. I started my career as a Fleet Street journalist years ago, and then TV. So very soon I'll need a sports reporter and I know from Sully that you used to be a journalist in Sri Lanka. You could report on all the sport. Big job. And then we'll need a cultural reporter and someone to handle marketing. I know that you, Mrs Rao, are a writer for some Indian presses and online journals."

"Yes, I am," Mum said.

"How would you like a full-time chief reporter's job and a column? Food, fashion, arts, culture, politics, whatever."

"I'd love to do it," Mum said. "But are you sure, Callista? I hope very much you're not just doing it because of all the business that went on with Mr Christaki?"

"I can't think of anyone better. I start preparations and buying things today, and we move into the offices in a few days. You know the reporter, Joanna, who pulled the whole thing off? The girl in the fedora? I've offered her the job of chief director. We need someone with her skills!"

"She'd be perfect," I exclaimed.

"I thought in the first edition we'd start with a splash," Callista went on. "Exclusives with Suleiman and Suleikha, Leo and Kai. A national scoop! Christaki and his Freezies."

"Drink?" Dad asked.

And that's what they did. The online paper was named *The Three Cheers Post*—a mad name, but then with Miss Callista Barr as editor, what did one expect? And with her connections, the ads tumbled in. She said it was making money before it even started.

When Mr C—Suleiman—wrote to the UK people to adopt Miriam properly, now that she had been granted asylum too, they wrote back saying that adoption rules specified that a child should be accommodated in a stable household, preferably of two partners.

"That's a very difficult one," Mr C said and scratched his head.

And just then, Miss Honey pulled up in her car.

**FARRUKH DHONDY** is a highly acclaimed British Indian author, dramatist and screenwriter. His latest books include *Prophet of Love, Rumi: A New Collection* and an autobiography entitled *Fragments against My Ruin: A Life*. He is a recipient of numerous prizes, including the prestigious Whitbread Book Award for his novel *Bombay Duck*. He lives in London, England.

The publisher thanks Karim Alrawi for his editorial advice.

LIBRARY AND ARCHIVES CANADA CATALOGUING IN PUBLICATION

TITLE: THE FREEZIES / FARRUKH DHONDY.
NAMES: DHONDY, FARRUKH, AUTHOR.
IDENTIFIERS: CANADIANA (PRINT) 20230552439 | CANADIANA (EBOOK) 20230552536 | ISBN 9781990598272
(SOFTCOVER) | ISBN 9781990598289 (EPUB)
SUBJECTS: LCGFT: NOVELS.
CLASSIFICATION: LCC PZ7.D45 FRE 2023 | DDC J823/.914—DC23

Book design by Elisa Gutiérrez

The text is set in Georgia Pro. Titles are set in Brushberry Sans One.

10  9  8  7  6  5  4  3  2  1

Printed and bound in Canada. The paper in this book came from
Forest Stewardship Certified and Sustainable Forestry Initiative fibers.

The publisher thanks the Government of Canada, the Canada Council for the Arts and Livres Canada Books for their financial support. We also thank the Government of the Province of British Columbia for the financial support we have received through the Book Publishing Tax Credit program and the British Columbia Arts Council.

Supported by the Province of British Columbia